New York New Delhi
Mexico City New Delhi

ACKNOWLEDGMENTS

Thank you to Nicole Betancourt, Olivia Branch, David Jacobs, Teri Granger Martin, Manuela Soares, and Adriana X. Tatum for their insightful reading of this story and helpful editorial suggestions. Thanks, also, to Jazan Higgins for help with astrology and Ari Moore for answering my questions on body piercing.

ISBN 0-439-49840-6

3 4 5 6 7 8/0

12 11 10 9 8 7 6 5 4 3 2

40

Book design by Joyce White.

Printed in the U.S.A.
First printing, November 2003

TABLE OF CONTENTS

DOWNTOWN

Empire State Bldg. ★
Washington Sq. Park
Youth Media Center ▲
City Hall
Joy's dad's block J D
WTC site

EAST RIVER

NEW JERSEY

HUDSON RIVER

11th Ave.
10th Ave.
9th Ave.
8th Ave.
7th Ave.
6th Ave.
5th Ave.

Broadway

34th St.

23rd St.

17th St.

14th St.

Chelsea

Greenwich Village

8th St.
4th St.

3rd Ave.
2nd Ave.
1st Ave.

East Village

E. Houston St.

Little Italy

W. Houston St.

Soho

Tribeca

Canal St.

Chinatown

West Broadway
Church St.
Broadway
Lafayette

Chambers St.
J D

Battery Park

BROOKLYN

Statue of Liberty

MANHATTAN IN NYC

Scale: 1 mile

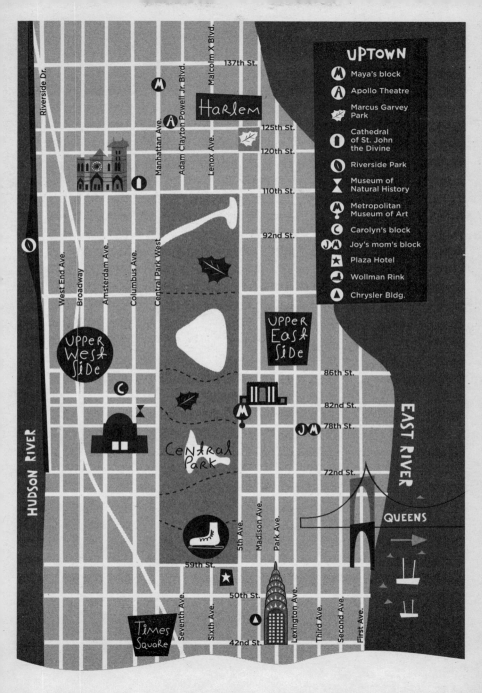

Astor Place

Joy checked herself out in the closet door mirror. Purple T-shirt and faded jeans. Check. Black boots. Check. Short leather jacket. Check. Black hair — short and sleek. Check. Matte pink lipstick.

Turning from the mirror, Joy put her digital camera in her backpack. She had agreed to take pictures for wanna-be-model Jay-Cee. She hadn't really felt like doing it. Jay-Cee wasn't her friend. All she knew about her was that she was totally into how she looked and wanted to be a model. But Jay-Cee was Maya's friend, and Maya was Joy's friend. So Joy had agreed to take the pictures — even though she knew *nothing* about shooting pictures for a modeling portfolio.

Two fashion magazines lay on Joy's bed. They'd given her a couple of ideas for the shoot. The background is important, she'd decided. And the model usually doesn't smile. Joy picked up the magazines to return them to Sue.

Her stepmother was doing sit-ups on the living room floor. Joy's baby half brother, Jake, was trying to pull himself up to stand at the coffee table. When Joy came in, Jake — momentarily distracted — dropped down on his diaper-padded bottom. He looked up at Joy and wailed.

"It wasn't *my* fault," she protested.

Sue stopped mid-sit-up to see what had happened.

"Jake's having trouble getting up," Joy explained. She pointed to the magazines. "I'm returning them."

As Sue helped Jake back up, she glanced at the magazines and grinned at Joy. "I love that you're *finally* interested in fashion," she said. "We have to go shopping together sometime soon. It will be such fun. We'll both get something new and trendy."

Joy didn't bother to tell Sue that she hadn't looked at the magazines for what was new and trendy. She was interested in photography. Sort of. Anyway, she was more interested than she was before she took the photo workshop last summer.

"Bye," she called as she opened the door.

"Don't forget you're baby-sitting for Jake tonight," Sue called back. "We're going to the opera."

Baby-sitting again, thought Joy as she closed the door. What a bore!

After the photo shoot with Jay-Cee, Joy was going to the first session of Photo Workshop 2. She'd finally see Carolyn and Maya again. By the end of Workshop 1 the three of them were pretty tight. But everyone had gone her own way when the workshop was over. Carolyn went back to Wyoming to visit her grandparents and friends. She'd sent Joy a card with a photograph of the family horse ranch.

While Carolyn was gone, Maya hadn't called Joy — not once. Joy had been away for part of the time. Two long weeks at the beach with her father, his wife, and the crybaby. But Maya could have reached me there, she thought. I had my cell phone.

As soon as Joy was back in the city, the school year started. Joy went to the same uptown private girls' school she'd gone to since kindergarten. Maya and Carolyn went to an alternative public junior high that Maya's grandmother started.

Maya had finally called yesterday to make sure Joy was still going to the photo workshop. It had been at least six weeks since the three girls had seen one another. Joy wondered if they'd still — all three — be friends. Or would she be left out, now that Carolyn and Maya went to school together?

"Hey, girl, wait up!"

Maya slowed down. Delores pulled up on one side of her, Shana on the other. They were Rollerblading around Central Park.

"Where's the fire?" asked Shana.

"Sorry. I was daydreaming," admitted Maya.

"About a bo-oy?" teased Shana.

Maya shook her head. "Uh-uh." She wasn't going to let on that Shana had guessed right. Anyway, she wasn't thinking about a boy the way Shana meant it. She was just wondering about Serge. He had appeared in her life so mysteriously last summer — taking her discarded newspapers and agreeing to let her photograph him. She'd first noticed him because of the piercings in his face and his purple streaked hair.

Shana skated backward in front of Maya. "Let's go to the movies this afternoon."

"I have photo workshop," Maya reminded her. "It starts today."

Shana came to a screeching stop. "Again? How come you didn't say?"

Delores pulled up beside them. "Saturday afternoons. She did say."

Shana shot Maya a hard look. "You didn't say so from what I heard."

"Yes I did," protested Maya. "When I told you I'd skate this morning." She looked around. They were still on the East Side. "I'm getting out of the park at Seventy-seventh Street. On the West Side."

"You still have to baby-sit that redhead?" mocked Shana. "Take her on the big ole scary subway?"

Maya didn't bother to tell Shana that Carolyn could go to the workshop alone now. That today she was going to meet up with Carolyn only because she wanted to. That would just make Shana angrier. Maya wondered if Jay-Cee had told Shana that Joy was taking her pictures. Would that bother Shana, too?

Maya looked up. The leaves on the trees were just beginning to turn autumn colors. The sky was a vibrant blue. She took her camera out of her backpack and aimed it upward.

Gold and red leaves against the blue sky. Click.

* * *

Carolyn pulled her warm clothes out of the dryer and dropped them in the laundry basket. She glanced up at the clock over the row of washing machines. 11:30. Maya was meeting her at noon. She'd better hurry. A woman at the other dryer held up a pink-and-white-checkered sock and asked, "Is this yours?"

"Yes, thank you," Carolyn answered as she reached for the sock.

"Pretty sock," the woman said.

Carolyn smiled. "They're my favorite socks." She rolled the two checkered socks together. "I'm always just losing one sock. It drives me crazy."

"There's a big pile of all those running-away socks someplace," the woman said with a grin.

As Carolyn left the laundry room she thought, Dad told me not to talk to strangers. To keep to myself. But people are so friendly in New York City. Even strangers. I love it. She opened the elevator door, stepped in, and pressed ten. As the elevator went up, Carolyn looked down at the checkered socks on top of her laundry. Her mother had picked out those socks for her the last time they'd gone clothes shopping together. She didn't ever want to lose them.

The elevator stopped at the first floor.

A young woman got on with the biggest dog Carolyn had ever seen and — possibly — the smallest. Carolyn picked up her basket to make room for them. The woman wore baggy jeans, a guy's basketball jacket, and her dark brown hair in a crew cut.

5

"Sorry," she said as they crowded into the elevator. "Precious takes up a lot of space."

Carolyn smiled to herself about the big dog's name and squinched into the corner. "That's okay."

The top of Precious's head reached her chest. He was about the height of her first pony.

"Your dogs are uh — interesting," commented Carolyn.

The woman rubbed the big dog's head. "They aren't mine. But I love Precious like he is mine." The small dog suddenly let out a jealous bark. "You, too, Max. I love all my dogs." She smiled over at Carolyn. "My name is Ivy. I walk six dogs in your building."

"All at once?" asked Carolyn in amazement.

"Sometimes," said Ivy.

The elevator stopped at ten and the doors opened. Carolyn squeezed around Precious to get out. "I've never seen a dog that big before."

"I've never seen hair as red as yours before," said Ivy. "I mean, that's natural. You're lucky." The doors closed between them.

Carolyn was used to people commenting on her hair. When she lived at home in Wyoming, folks said, "You got your mother's gorgeous red hair." But her mother got cancer and had to have an operation and then chemotherapy. Because of the chemo, she lost all her hair. When the chemo treatments were over, her hair started to grow back. It was as red as ever. But before long, her mother was sick again and back on chemo. Then she died.

Carolyn wanted to tell her mom about the big dog she'd just seen. Tears welled up in her eyes. She wanted to tell her mother so many things. She wiped the tears away with the checkered socks. Through the apartment door she heard her father laughing. Is Maya here already? she wondered. She walked in and saw that he was talking on the phone. Seeing her, he quickly ended the call.

"Cake's in the oven," he announced.

"Laundry's out of the drier!" she called back.

Carolyn took the laundry basket to her room and made her bed with the clean sheets. The smell of the chocolate cake baking reached her. They'd been invited to Maya's for dinner that night, and her father was bringing the dessert. She came back to the main room of the apartment — living room, dining area, kitchen — all in one not-very-big room.

"The cake smells great," she told him.

"I hope everyone at Maya's likes chocolate," he said.

The doorbell rang. Carolyn opened the door and Maya rolled in. "*Everyone* at Maya's *adores* chocolate," she said as she glided up to the counter.

"I beg your pardon?" said Mr. Kuhlberg.

"Sorry," said Maya. She sat on a stool and started to undo her Rollerblades. "My mother hates when I skate in the house, too."

"I didn't mean the skating," he said. "I just wondered, did you hear what I said about chocolate *through* the door? Even before Carolyn opened it?"

Maya thought for a second. "Yeah. I guess I did."

He looked at Carolyn. "Could you hear what I was saying on the phone before you came in?"

"I heard you laughing," she said. "Why? Who were you talking to?"

"Someone from work," he said. "But some of my work is confidential."

Her father was an entomologist who specialized in cockroaches. "Confidential about cockroaches?" Carolyn asked as she tried to hold back a grin.

Her father forced a scowl. "Yes, some of it is *highly* confidential." The oven timer buzzed. "And not a laughing matter."

Carolyn thought, You were laughing on the phone. But she said, "Sorry, Dad."

Maya was putting on her sneakers. "We better get going or we'll be late on the first day. Can I leave my Rollerblades here?"

"Sure," agreed Carolyn. "I'll bring them tonight when we come for dinner." She picked up the skates and spun the front wheel. It would be fun to Rollerblade. At home, she'd spent all her free time with her horse, Tailgate, and riding with her friends. Now she wasn't riding and had time to Rollerblade. Her mother would have encouraged her to take up a new sport. But her supercautious father said it was too dangerous.

"Look this way," Joy instructed Jay-Cee. She had started the shoot by taking photos of Jay-Cee near an outdoor café on Eighth Street. Now she posed her against a big, balancing cube sculpture at the intersection of Astor Place, Eighth Street, and Fourth Avenue. Joy took a picture and checked it out in the screen. Jay-Cee's golden-brown skin glowed against the matte black background of the cube.

"Right hip forward, hands behind your head," instructed Joy. *Click.*

"Lean toward me." *Click.*

People were rushing to and fro in the background. Good, Joy thought. It gives the shots a hurried, urban look.

"Stand with your legs far apart. Now pout. That's it." *Click.*

"Turn around. Hands on hips. Look over your shoulder at me." *Click.* "Ex-cel-lent." *Click.*

Two passersby suddenly jumped into the frame on either side of Jay-Cee and grinned at the camera.

Maya, Jay-Cee, and Carolyn, grinning. Click.

Joy turned the camera off and went to them.

"Hi, Joy," said Carolyn cheerfully. "I haven't seen you in forever. I'm so excited that we're taking class together again! We'll have so much fun."

"Yeah," said Joy. "I hope so." She'd forgotten how perky Carolyn could be.

"How you doing, Joy?" asked Maya. "Everything okay? With your stepmother and everything?"

"Sure," answered Joy. She'd also forgotten how nosy Maya could be. Still, it felt oddly good to be with these two again. They were a lot better than the girls in her classes at school.

"Joy took some *fab*-u-lous pictures for me," gushed Jay-Cee as she struck a mocking glam pose.

A man passing by gave Jay-Cee the once-over and muttered, "Hot mama."

It gave Joy the creeps when guys said stuff like that to her. But it didn't seem to bother Jay-Cee. She just ignored it. Joy checked her watch. "We better go," she said. "Beth would be rudely annoyed if we're late."

Carolyn almost said, "Beth isn't rude," but stopped herself. Joy liked to be negative. And sarcastic. That was just her way. Sometimes it was funny. Sometimes it wasn't.

A few minutes later, the three girls walked into the Youth Media Center. Beth Bernstein was laying photographs out on a long table. Maya glanced around the room to check out who else was taking the workshop. There were seven other kids. Three were talking in a tight group. They obviously already knew one another. The rest of the kids were looking at the photographs on the table.

Maya recognized only two kids from their summer workshop, Janice and Charlie. During that workshop, Charlie had told the class he had some condition that would probably make him blind in a few years. He already wore really thick lenses. He said he was taking photography because he wanted to see as much as he could while he could. Maya was impressed that he didn't seem to feel sorry for himself. Janice was okay, too. Maya liked the photos she took. They were very artsy.

"Hi, you three," said Beth with a glance at the clock. "Glad you could make it."

Beth is as sarcastic as Joy, thought Carolyn.

"Let's begin, everyone," she announced. "We'll start by walking around the table looking at some photos. In five minutes we'll talk about them. Pick out the one that interests you the most and think about what you'll say about it. You can introduce yourselves to one another then, too. But keep it zipped for now."

The first photo Carolyn noticed was of a horribly wounded child in front of a bombed-out building. She looked away.

Joy had noticed it, too. But she didn't look away. She studied it. Nothing in the photo told you where it was taken. That's what was so interesting about it. The innocent victim of violence. Things like this were happening in so many places in the world right now. It was the photo she'd talk about.

Maya made her choice. She'd talk about the picture of a young black girl in a white dress, with schoolbooks, walking past an angry mob of white people. She knew the picture. Her grandmother had shown it to her. It was a powerful photo. The composition and the angle were perfect for the subject. That's what she'd talk about.

Carolyn still hadn't chosen a photo. But her eyes kept roaming back to one of a bird in shallow water, its legs caught up in the plastic rings of a six-pack holder. She remembered a trail ride with her mother. They'd come across a horse caught in a tangle of barbed wire that someone had carelessly left in the corner of a fenced-in field. They were able to free the horse. Did the person who took the bird photo free it after taking the shot? she wondered.

"Everyone take a seat," instructed Beth. "Let's talk. Then I'll give you your assignment. You'll have the full ten weeks to do it."

Maya wondered how the assignment was connected with the photos on the table.

Carolyn took out her notebook and pen so she could write down the assignment exactly.

Joy rolled her eyes and sighed. This was too much like school.

"When I say *assignment*," continued Beth, "I'm using a newspaper term. Reporters and photographers are sent out on *assignment*. You're given an *assignment*." She looked right at Joy. "So let's not get all bent out of shape like this is just another school-type thing you're burdened with. Besides, you're all here of your own free will. No one *has* to take these classes."

If everyone quits, thought Joy, you don't have a job.

An hour later the three girls left the workshop together.

"I like it that we're only doing one big assignment for this workshop," observed Maya.

"Actually there are *three* assignments," corrected Joy. "First, we have to take snapshots of subjects we might want to do for the big assignment. Second, we have to do that photo diary thing —"

"That's to explore our ideas for the big project," interrupted Carolyn. "I think I'm going to like that part."

They stepped outside.

"But it's a *separate* thing we have to do," insisted Joy. "Then there's the final assignment to explore our chosen subject with a camera. Three assignments. And she'll probably give us more later on. She said."

They walked out of the media center. Joy saw Maya roll her eyes at Carolyn. Do they hate that I said that? she wondered. Was I acting too much like a know-it-all? Do I sound like a complainer?

A fresh-smelling autumn breeze blew past Carolyn. Two women in saris walked by. Across the street, girls were jumping rope to a rhyme.

"There are so many things that interest me in New York that I don't know if I can pick just one thing for the project," said Carolyn.

"Lucky you," said Joy.

Don't be hurt, Carolyn told herself. Just give it back to her. She grinned at Joy mischievously. "I'll share. You can have my leftover ideas."

Joy grinned at her. "Thanks. I'll keep that in mind if I get desperate."

"I already know what I want to do," announced Maya.

"You got an idea so quick?" said Carolyn.

"I actually had this idea the first day of the summer workshop," Maya remembered, "when I saw Serge for the first time."

"You already took pictures of him," Joy reminded her.

"Maybe she's going to do more photos — like how he came from Russia and is learning English," said Carolyn.

"How do you show that in photos?" asked Joy.

"With little word balloons," joked Carolyn.

"I don't want to do Serge again," explained Maya. "I want to take pictures in a piercing parlor. Maybe show someone getting pierced."

What a disgusting idea, thought Joy.

Does Maya want to be pierced? wondered Carolyn.

Maya looked up the block. "There are a lot of those piercing places around here. Let's go look at some. I'll take snapshots — just from the outside — to show in the workshop next week."

"Okay," agreed Carolyn.

I'd rather go have a soda or something, thought Joy, but she didn't say so. When Maya wanted to do something, there was no holding her back.

Walking east, the girls passed boutiques specializing in handbags, fabrics from India, and jewelry. In the next block there was one Thai, one Greek, and two Italian restaurants, a barbershop offering a sale on buzz cuts, and four opportunities to have your body tattooed or pierced. Maya took out her camera in front of the last piercing parlor.

A display of body jewelry and antiseptic lotions. Click.

A guy with tattoos on his arms and neck walking past. Click.

This place is so grungy, thought Joy. The displays are dusty, and the inside looks messy. I'd never go in there.

Carolyn felt for her silver stud earrings. She'd had her ears pierced in Hanson's Jewelers in downtown Dubois. It was *nothing* like this place.

Maya moved in for a close-up. *A cluster of five belly rings. Click.*

"It doesn't look very sanitary," observed Carolyn.

"Shana had a belly ring that got infected," said Maya. "Maybe she had it done in a place like this. It got gross. All pus-sy and everything."

"What'd her mother say?" asked Carolyn.

Maya put her camera back in the pack. "Her mother didn't notice."

Maya didn't tell Carolyn and Joy that Shana's mother didn't notice much of anything about Shana. She looked through the store window. The woman working behind the counter and the two customers in there looked tough and a lot older than she was. How would they feel about her taking their pictures? Did she have the nerve to walk in and just ask to do that?

"Do you think the place Serge works is like this?" Carolyn wondered out loud.

"I hope not," exclaimed Maya.

Serge, thought Joy. She remembered the odd but handsome boy and how he took Maya's newspapers when she left them carefully on the edge of trash cans in the subway station. As a joke, they'd started leaving notes for him in the newspapers. He seemed to really like Maya, and she'd been the one to take pictures of him for the workshop. He'd even come to their photography exhibit at the end of the workshop. It felt like Maya, Carolyn, and I were great friends that night, thought Joy. But are we? "Has Serge called you or anything?" she asked Maya.

"No." Maya thought out loud. "If he still works in a piercing place, maybe I could check it out."

Joy looked up at the street signs. They were on Sixth Street near the corner of Avenue A. "He lives with his uncle someplace on Avenue A," she observed.

"His uncle's a super," Carolyn remembered. "He said it was a big building."

"Serge took the train at Eighth Street," put in Maya. "So his uncle's building is probably on Avenue A around here."

"If we can figure out what building it is, we can leave Serge a note," suggested Carolyn.

"In a newspaper," added Joy.

"Yes!" agreed Carolyn.

"But what are we going to say?" asked Maya.

Harlem

Maya pointed to a display of newspapers on the street near them.

"Free newspapers. Perfect." She opened a copy of the *Village Voice* to the centerfold and laid it on top of the newspaper dispenser. Carolyn handed her a red felt-tipped pen.

"Now what should I say?" mused Maya.

"How about 'Wanted. Metal Guy with connections'?" suggested Joy.

Maya tapped the pen against her forehead. "That might work."

Carolyn didn't say anything. Joy turned to her. "You don't like it?"

Carolyn shook her head. "Maya is asking him to do her a favor. I don't think it should be funny or sarcastic. I think it should be — courteous."

"Like Please and May I?" teased Joy.

"Maybe I should be more direct," Maya said, looking at Carolyn. "Right?"

Carolyn nodded.

Maya pulled open the pen. She wrote, HI, SERGE. IT'S MAYA. I NEED YOUR HELP WITH ANOTHER PHOTOGRAPHY

ASSIGNMENT. IT'S NOT A BIG DEAL, I DON'T THINK. COULD YOU? WOULD YOU? IF THE ANSWER IS YES OR MAYBE, CALL ME AT 212-555-5610. MAYA.

She looked from Joy to Carolyn. "Do you guys want to add something?"

"Just that I said hi," Carolyn told her.

"And that I said to have a nice day," added Joy. She arched an eyebrow in Carolyn's direction and half-smiled. Their first message to Serge was "Have a nice day." It was Carolyn's idea. Joy and Maya had meant it sarcastically, as a joke, because it was such an overused expression. Carolyn had meant it sincerely.

Maya and I were really in sync that day, thought Joy. Now Maya and Carolyn are the ones in sync, and I'm the one left out.

Carolyn remembered how hurt she was by Joy's sarcasm when they first met. Now that she knew Joy, she didn't mind her sarcasm so much. Sometimes she even liked it.

"We should put what Joy said at the top of the page," Carolyn said. "In bigger print. Like a headline."

Maya studied the page of newsprint, covered now with her red-inked message. "That'll work," she agreed. She wrote, WANTED: METAL GUY WITH CONNECTIONS.

They started their search for Serge's uncle's building on Avenue A between Seventh and Eighth streets.

Joy pointed to the largest apartment building on the block. "Let's try that building first," she suggested.

They went into the entryway, and Maya ran her finger down the row of buzzers. She stopped on the one labeled SUPERINTENDENT and pressed.

"What?" crackled a voice over the intercom.

"Does Serge live here?" Maya asked, suddenly embarrassed not to know his last name.

"Serge is at work," answered the voice. "Not here."

"Maybe he's at the piercing place," Carolyn whispered to Joy.

Maya leaned closer to the intercom. "I just want to leave him something. A newspaper."

"Okay. Yes. Leave it. Later I get."

Maya quickly scribbled SERGE in big letters across the front page of the paper and put it on the floor near the door. The girls went back out on the street. They grinned at one another.

It's just like last summer, thought Joy. Fun with friends. "Want to get a slice or something?" she asked.

"We have to go," Maya and Carolyn answered together.

Joy looked from one to the other, surprised that they spoke in unison.

"My dad and I are going to Maya's for dinner," Carolyn explained.

Maya saw the hurt in Joy's eyes and realized that she felt left out.

"Can you come, too?" she asked Joy. "My grandmother's cooking, which means there will be some fine-tasting food. Can you? Do you want to?"

"I can't," Joy said. She spotted a cab and hailed

it. "I have to baby-sit tonight." Why did Maya ask her at the last minute like that? Why didn't she ask her when she asked Carolyn? The cab pulled up and she got in.

"I'll let you know if Newspaper Boy calls," Maya shouted to her. But the cab door was already closed.

Carolyn sat between Maya and her grandmother, Josie. Her father was across the table from her. He was talking about the conference on insects that he'd be attending in Thailand. Carolyn smiled to herself and thought, I'll be staying with Maya for ten whole days while he's gone. It's going to be so much fun.

"I'm going to do my science project for school about spiders," Maya's nine-year-old sister, Hannah, announced. She gave Mr. Kuhlberg's shirtsleeve a little tug. "Will you help me?"

"Hannah!" scolded Mrs. Johnson. "Don't be troubling Mr. Kuhlberg with that. He doesn't have time —"

"It's no trouble," Mr. Kuhlberg protested. "Sounds like Hannah is an entomologist in the making. I'd like to help her. It's one more for our side." He smiled across the table at Carolyn. "I used to help Carolyn with her science projects." He turned back to Hannah.

Maya leaned toward Carolyn. "Your dad's so relaxed. Is that what he was like before your mother — when your mother was alive?"

Carolyn remembered her dad helping her with her science projects, making her birthday cakes, reading her stories, teaching her how to play chess, laughing with her and her mom. That was one side of her dad. But the other side was her strict dad who was scared she'd get hurt and who worried over little things. "Some of the time he was like that," she told Maya. "More than he is now."

From where she sat, Carolyn could see Maya's parents in the kitchen, getting plates for the cake. Mr. Johnson put a hand on his wife's shoulder and whispered in her ear. She turned and planted a kiss on his cheek. My mom and dad were like that, too, she thought. But she couldn't tell Maya because of the lump in her throat.

"Do you think your dad would let you stay over tonight?" whispered Maya.

Carolyn grinned. "Maybe. You ask."

Maya popped the question after everyone had ooh-ed and aah-ed over Mr. Kuhlberg's chocolate cake. As soon as he said yes, Maya remembered Shana. Most Sunday mornings, Shana came over. What would she think when she saw Carolyn there?

"Jake, why are you crying?" Joy demanded. He answered her with a howl of unhappiness. She held him above her head and jiggled him. But Jake didn't squeal happily the way he did for their dad. He only cried louder.

As she lowered Jake, she caught a whiff of smelly diaper. She wrinkled her nose. "Phew. That stinks!" She put him down on his changing table and went to work. "Why do you wait until they're gone to poop?" she asked in a friendly enough voice. "You think I want to change your messy diapers?" she continued. "You know I hate that you do that. Is that why you do it?" He'd stopped crying and was listening to her. So she kept talking. She told him what she'd done at the workshop, what opera his parents had gone to see, when they would be home, and how she had missed going to Maya's because of him. As she powdered his behind, she noticed that he was unusually warm. She spread her whole hand over his belly. "You're hot." She leaned over and kissed his forehead. It was warmer than she'd ever felt it. And he was crying again.

It wasn't his "I'm hungry" cry or the "I want attention" cry. It was a new cry, one that said, "I'm in pain." And it frightened her. She patted the tabs of his diaper in place and asked, "What's wrong, Jake? Are you sick?"

The phone rang. She picked him up and went for it. Jake dropped his head on her shoulder and pulled on his ear. The heat of his little body seeped through her shirt and into her skin. "Hello," Joy said into the receiver, hoping it was her father.

"Hi." It wasn't her father. It was Maya. "Guess what? Serge called, and he's going to meet us at that piercing parlor where he works. Saturday. He'll introduce me to the owner. This guy named Ivan. After the workshop. And listen to this, the place is called Zeus. It's definitely not one of those we already saw. So you'll come with us on Saturday, right?"

"Yeah. Sure. Whatever," said Joy. "I have to go. The baby's sick. I think he's got a fever."

He started crying again.

"Did you take his temperature?" asked Maya.

Joy carried Jake and the phone over to the shelf where Sue kept baby supplies. She found the thermometer. "I've never taken his temperature before," she admitted into the phone.

Maya told her to put the thermometer under his armpit. Jake pulled on his ear again and whimpered.

"He's rubbing his ear a lot," Joy observed. "And pulling on it. Do you think he has an earache?"

"Probably," answered Maya. "That's so painful. You should call your parents. And call us later to let us know what happens." She paused. "Carolyn is staying over."

Joy was too worried about Jake to really care.

She was about to dial her father's cell phone when she remembered that it would be turned off for the opera.

She put Jake back on the changing table to check the thermometer. It read 103 degrees. She picked him back up. He wasn't crying anymore. He wasn't even looking at her. He just lay there, listlessly rubbing at his ears, a deadweight in her arms.

Her heart pounded, and she suddenly felt hot herself — with fear. What if something awful happened to Jake? She'd heard that people could have convulsions if their temperatures went too high. What was too high? Or what if he suddenly stopped breathing?

I have to call 911, she thought. I have to get help. The phone, which was lying next to Jake's head, rang again. He was startled. Alert again to his pain, he wailed. Joy saw in the caller ID window that the call was from her father's cell phone. "Jake's sick," she said into the phone — almost crying herself. "He's got a temperature of 103."

Sue was on the other end. "We're on our way," she said. "We'll be there in fifteen minutes."

Joy walked around the apartment with the hot, limp baby. "Your mommy and daddy are coming home," she cooed. "They'll know what to do. You're going to be all right."

An image flashed in her head. When she was little and had a fever, her mother put a cool wet washcloth on her forehead. She put Jake in his crib and quickly wet one of his baby washcloths. When her dad and stepmother came in, Joy was sitting on the couch patting Jake's hot body with it.

Sue rushed over and reached for him.

"I think he has an earache," Joy said as she handed Jake over. "I was just putting —"

Sue turned to her husband. "He's burning up. We better put him in a tepid bath."

"I'll get the fever medicine," he offered.

Half an hour later, Jake's fever was going down, and he was sleeping fitfully in his father's arms. But he was still rubbing his ears.

"I'm taking him in to the pediatrician first thing in the morning," Sue commented. "He was cranky this afternoon, and I thought he felt a little warm."

So why did you leave him with me? thought Joy.

They didn't even thank me. Or say they were sorry for leaving me with their sick baby.

She went back to the kitchen fridge and served herself a dish of double chocolate-chip ice cream.

Sue came in and glanced at the mound of ice cream. "Are you sure you want that?" she asked. "You could have some frozen yogurt or fruit instead."

Joy ignored her skinny, calorie-counting step-mother and went to her room — with the ice cream.

At seven o'clock on Friday nights, Carolyn and her father went out for Chinese food. Her father loved routine. "There's a time and place for everything," was one of his favorite, often-repeated sayings. He'd decided that their time for Chinese food was Friday nights and the place was Silk Road Palace. Other nights of the week, they ate at home. Sunday — baked chicken, rice, and broccoli. Monday — fish fillets, potatoes, and string beans. On Tuesdays, it was pizza — delivered — and salad — made at home. And so on. "It makes grocery shopping easier," her father reasoned. "You use the same shopping list every week."

As they were walking out of the building, headed for Chinese at Silk Road Palace, Ivy and Precious were coming into the building.

"Hey, Carolyn," Ivy said as the two pairs approached one another. "How's it going?"

"Fine," answered Carolyn. Precious came up to her. She patted his head.

"Don't touch a strange dog," her father muttered in her ear.

"It's all right, Dad," Carolyn assured him as she rubbed the dog's big silky ear. "Precious isn't a stranger. I met him last week." She smiled at Ivy. "This is Ivy. She's a dog walker."

"But mostly I'm a musician," corrected Ivy. "A percussionist." She tapped a beat out on her leg as if to prove the point.

Carolyn gestured toward her father. "This is my dad."

"Donald Kuhlberg," he said.

Ivy extended a hand to shake. "Ivy George." Carolyn noticed a tattoo encircling her wrist. It looked like barbed wire.

"If you ever need a dog walker — or a percussionist — I'm your person," she said as she made a little wave and walked to the elevator.

On the way to the restaurant, Carolyn's father asked questions about Ivy: "How did you meet that woman? . . . Who spoke first? . . . Did you see that tattoo on her wrist? . . . Why do people disfigure themselves like that?" While they waited for their order, he reminded her not to talk to strangers.

"I won't," she promised.

The waiter reached in front of her and put down two dishes. "One order sesame noodles. One order steam dumpling," he announced. "Chopsticks?"

She and her dad both took chopsticks and smiled at each other. The food smelled delicious.

While Carolyn wrapped sesame noodles around chopsticks, she thought, Ivy's not a stranger anymore. I've talked to her two times. She wondered about Ivy. What were the other dogs like that she walked? Where did she drum? Was she in a band or did she play alone? Ivy seemed so independent and unique. An idea flashed in Carolyn's head. She could do her photojournalism project on her. "Perfect," she heard herself say out loud.

"What's perfect?" her father asked.

"The sesame noodles," she answered. "They're exactly the way I like them."

"That's the value of going to the same place every week," he said, smiling.

Friday was changeover day for Joy. She threw her suitcase in the trunk of the cab. It had been a long week at her father's. Jake was finally better, but he'd been cranky for days with the earache.

After school, Sue kept turning to her for help. "Joy, will you just watch Jake while I run down and buy something for dinner?"

"Joy, could you just watch him while I take a nap?"

"If only I could go to yoga I know I'd feel better. Could you watch him?"

It was hard to keep up with her schoolwork with all the interruptions. When she stayed at her dad's, she had to take the subway to and from school. That meant getting up an hour earlier than when she was at her mother's. Living downtown and going to school uptown was a drag. Going back and forth between her parents' apartments was a drag. Keeping track of her stuff in two places was a drag.

Joy leaned back in the cab and closed her eyes. It would be such a relief to be at her mother's — back to the room that had been hers for as long as she could remember. It was quiet there, and she could do what she wanted, when she wanted.

If I were uptown all the time, I'd be only a couple of blocks from school — and closer to Maya and Carolyn, she thought. If only I could just live uptown. Why can't I just live where I want?

When her parents first separated and decided on joint custody and sharing her equally, her uncle Brett had asked her if that's what *she* wanted. She'd nodded solemnly and said, "I want to be with my mommy *and* my daddy. I want to live in two places." Uncle Brett had leaned over and kissed the top of her head. "Then that's what you'll do, honey," he'd promised.

She wished she could tell him that she'd changed her mind and didn't want to live in two places anymore. That she only wanted to live at her mom's. But Uncle Brett was dead, and there wasn't anyone else to tell.

The cab turned on to her block. "The third building in on the right," she told the cabbie as she pulled out her wallet to pay him.

As Joy was swinging her suitcase out of the

trunk, a voice inside her said, *You should be able to live where you want. Tell them.*

The doorman was beside her, reaching for the suitcase. "I'll take that, Miss Benoit," he said. She had never bothered to tell him that her name was Benoit-Cohen, that she had both of her parents' last names.

Her mother was in the kitchen opening a bottle of wine. "There you are," she said cheerfully. "I just got in myself." She poured herself wine. "I'm celebrating. We landed a big Chanel perfume campaign for TV." Joy's mother's company — Benoit Productions — produced TV commercials for the fashion industry. Her job was to convince people in the fashion industry to let her company design and shoot their ad campaigns. "I'll have to work tomorrow. But that's okay with you, right? You're okay on your own?"

"Sure." Joy went to the refrigerator for some ginger ale. She'd been alone a lot in this apartment. Her mother handed her a wineglass for the soda. "I have photo workshop tomorrow, anyway. And I'm helping Maya with her project after."

Her mother pulled a folder of take-out menus from the drawer. "So we're both working." Alice Benoit took the few steps between herself and her daughter and kissed her on the cheek. "How are you, honey? How was everything at Baby Central this week?"

"Okay," answered Joy. "Sort of."

Her mother sat at the table. "What is that supposed to mean?"

Joy was going to explain about Jake being sick

but changed her mind. "I'm sick of going back and forth between two places. I want to live uptown full-time — near my school and near my friends."

Her mother arched an eyebrow. "You don't like living with your father? Is Ted hard to live with? Well, there's a surprise."

"It's not about Dad," she said, sitting down across from her mother.

Joy had learned early in the divorce not to complain about her father to her mother. And vice versa. It only made them angrier with each other and put her in the middle of it. She'd had enough of that when they were married.

"Oh?" her mother arched her eyebrow again. "The wife, then? And the kid. Are you sick of being their built-in baby-sitter?" She took a sip of wine. "Well, I found Ted impossible to live with, so why wouldn't you?"

"I'm just sick of living in two places, Mom," Joy said. "It's like I'm a Ping-Pong ball that you and Dad hit back and forth." She looked around the room, desperate for a way to make her plan work. "Will you ask him if I can stay here all the time? At least for the school year. Tell him about school and about my friends being up here."

Her mother looked at her. "You, my dear, will have to tell him — I mean *ask* him — yourself. And be sure he knows I have nothing to do with it. If I ask, he'll think we're doing Divorce Battle, Part Two. I don't think any of us could survive that."

She's right, thought Joy. I should ask him myself.

Alice flipped through the menus. "Sushi okay with you?"

"That's what I was thinking I wanted tonight," said Joy, pleased by the coincidence.

"I'm having sushi deluxe, then," her mother said. "What do you want?"

"The same, if you'll trade me your shrimp for my salmon rolls."

"It's a deal," her mother agreed. She put a hand over Joy's. "I'd be very glad to have you here all the time. You know that, don't you?"

Joy nodded. That's what she liked about living with her mother. They understood each other. If only her father would understand.

Wall Street

Carolyn walked out of the dark lobby into the noonday light. Before heading downtown to the photo workshop, she checked up and down the street to see if Ivy was around. She'd written about her idea to photograph Ivy. Now she needed snapshots of Ivy with the dogs and — more important — she needed to ask Ivy to be her subject. She spotted the silhouette of a large animal at the corner. Her heart started to race as she walked toward Ivy, Precious, and four other dogs. Under that beat, a calm voice coming from deep inside her whispered, *It's no big deal. Just ask her.*

"Hi there, Red," Ivy greeted her. "How's it going?"

Carolyn told her that she was looking for a subject for her photography project. "I thought maybe you'd make an interesting subject. Because you walk dogs and are a musician in New York City," she explained. "I'd need to take some snapshots and talk to the class about it. Then I'd take more pictures." She paused to catch her breath.

Ivy stared at her with an intense unsmiling gaze and bit her lower lip.

Carolyn felt herself blush. "Well, I have to go," she announced. "Sorry to bother you."

Ivy held up a hand. "Hold on, Red. I was just thinking about it. What I wonder is, would the dogs be in the pictures? If your photos are going to be in an exhibit or anything, maybe I should get their permission." She finally smiled. "Not the dogs' permission. The owners'. I'm sure they'll say yes, but I should ask."

"You'll do it?" Carolyn asked. "I can take your picture?" She was suddenly relaxed and excited — and smiling herself.

Precious sniffed Ivy's leg and looked up at her. She rubbed his head. "Yeah," said Ivy. "Why not?"

"No reason," answered Carolyn. "Can I take a few pictures now? We're supposed to do that to explore the subject."

"Explore away. But I can't pose right now." Ivy signaled the dogs it was time to go. "I've got to keep moving."

"I want action shots, anyway," Carolyn said as she turned to walk backward in front of Ivy and her canine charges.

Ivy walking down the block surrounded by five dogs. Click.

Close-up of Precious sniffing Ivy's hand. Click.

"You interested in pictures of me as a musician, too?" asked Ivy. "You know, with the band. I'm not just a dog walker."

"I was just going to ask you about that," said Carolyn, pleased that Ivy mentioned it first.

Shot from above: all the dogs around Ivy's legs and feet. Click.

"We're performing next Sunday — on Columbus Avenue — at the street fair," Ivy said. "There'll be a lot of different bands. Our set is from two-thirty to three."

"I'd love to come," exclaimed Carolyn. "That'll be perfect. What's your band called?"

"The Big Bang Band."

Close-up of Ivy smiling. Click.

Carolyn ran all the way to the subway. Her father's *"Don't run on the street"* was only a faint echo in her head.

Three hours later, Carolyn, Maya, and Joy left the media center together. A cool breeze blew Carolyn's hair. She was glad she'd worn her jean jacket.

Joy turned to Maya. "What's this Zeus piercing place like? Is it like those places we saw last week?"

"Serge just told me the address," answered Maya. "I couldn't exactly ask him if he works in a grungy place."

"Just because those places look grungy doesn't mean they aren't sanitary," commented Carolyn. "When they pierce your body, I mean."

Joy looked at her quizzically. "What are you saying?"

"I was thinking about our ranch," Carolyn explained. "You wouldn't like how it smells and how dirty everything gets. My boots get caked with mud. My clothes are either muddy or dusty, depending on the weather. My nails are always a mess. You would think it's grungy. But when we do stuff — like branding or inseminations — well, it's very sanitary."

Joy arched an eyebrow at her. "Inseminations?"

Maya pushed between them. "Could we just talk about what I'm going to say to Serge's boss?"

"How about asking him if they do branding there?" teased Joy. "Or inseminations."

"I was just trying to make a point," said Carolyn defensively.

"Sor-ry," said Joy. She saw the hurt in Carolyn's eyes and now really was sorry that she'd teased her.

Maya wondered if it was a mistake to bring Carolyn and Joy with her. Maybe she'd have been better off alone. Or with Shana, who had some experience with body piercing. Why hadn't she thought of asking Shana to go with her?

"Just be friendly," Carolyn suggested, interrupting Maya's thoughts and answering her original question.

"Maybe today you should just look around and see what the place is like," added Joy. "You can always call this guy later and ask about taking pictures. You might decide that you don't want to do piercing as your project."

"You're right," agreed Maya.

They stopped for a DON'T WALK signal before crossing Avenue B and Eighth Street. To get a head start, they stepped off the curb to wait for the light to change. A cab careening around the corner came so close to Carolyn that she felt a breeze.

"Whoa," exclaimed Joy as she pulled Carolyn out of the way.

"Never step off the curb until the light changes" was another of her father's "Rules for City Living" that Carolyn had been ignoring.

Half a block later, the girls saw ZEUS written in gold and black paint across a storefront window. A black banner above it commanded in silver: TATTOO IT. PIERCE IT. DO IT.

Joy looked at the window display and into the store. It was just like the ones they'd seen the week before — grungy.

Maya spotted Serge inside stocking a shelf. She knocked on the window. He didn't seem to hear her, but a girl behind the counter did and looked up. "What?" the girl mouthed, flashing a tongue pierced in two places. Maya pointed to Serge. The girl said something to him, and he finally looked up. Seeing Maya, he grinned broadly and waved for her to come in.

"Let's go," said Maya, more confident now that she'd made contact.

Serge met them at the door. "Hi, photo girls. How is everybody? Come on into my workplace."

Maya had forgotten how much she liked Serge's Russian accent. "How are your English classes?" she asked.

"Very excellent," he said. "I speak more and more English every day and soon I will be William Shakespeare."

Serge and Shakespeare, thought Joy. She imagined him, with his purple-streaked hair and piercings, acting in Shakespeare's play *Romeo and Juliet*.

Carolyn counted the jewelry in his face and was glad to see that it was holding steady at four piercings.

She also checked out the girl behind the counter. Her hair was irregularly cut, spiked, and bleached-dyed pink. Her nose and the dimpled space below it were pierced with silver studs. Nails and lips: black. So were her clothes. The girl's hands were on her hips. Multi-ringed fingers pointed to a barbell hanging from her belly button.

Carolyn thought about how she'd had to take off her belt for airport security because the buckle set off the metal detector. What would this girl have to take off to get through security?

"You going to introduce me to your school chums?" the clerk asked Serge.

"What is *chum*?" Serge whispered to Maya.

"Friends," she whispered back.

"Wren, these are my chums," Serge said. "They are not school chums, but friends only."

Wren rolled her eyes in response to his long explanation. The girls introduced themselves.

"Which one of you is getting done today?" Wren asked, already bored with them. "Or are you all doing some cute little friendship thing, like an itsy-bitsy daisy tattoo someplace where you hope your parents won't see it?"

Joy and Carolyn sneaked a glance at each other. What was this Wren girl's problem?

"We're here to see Ivan," Joy stated.

"He's in the back," Serge said. "I will bring you."

"Don't interrupt him," warned Wren. "He doesn't like that. He might go crazy with the staple gun."

Joy and Maya exchanged a look of alarm.

Serge laughed. "Wren jokes with the customer all the time," he explained.

"She's a barrel of laughs," Joy muttered to Carolyn.

Serge's knock on the office door was answered by, "It's open."

They all went into a small room that reminded Maya of her dentist's office — shiny and clean. In fact, the chair in the middle of the room looked just like her dentist's chair. Sharp instruments in a range of sizes lay in an orderly row near sterilizing equipment. A display of framed photos showed off examples of tattoos and piercings.

Piercings on *all* parts of the body, Carolyn noticed.

"Ivan, I introduce you to my chums who wanted to meet you and see where I work," Serge explained by way of introduction.

Ivan was darkly handsome in black jeans, cowboy boots, and a tight, sleeveless white T-shirt that showed off an array of tattoos.

Carolyn had to keep looking back at the photos on the wall so she wouldn't stare at his tattoos. Then back at the tattoos because some of those photos embarrassed her. Was that tattoo on Ivan's right arm a skull?

He had only one piercing that Maya could see — on his earlobe, where a large red jewel sparkled in the artificial light of the room.

"You're all too young," Ivan said. He looked Joy up and down. "Unless you're eighteen."

Joy shook her head *no* and looked at the floor to avoid his intense gaze.

Ivan turned to Serge. "You should have told them about the age thing." Looking back at the girls, he added, "A parent has to come with you, and there are forms to sign. It's the law."

Maya wondered who broke the law to give Shana her belly-button piercing. She glanced again at the neat row of needles and knives. It all seemed so medical here, but in a creepy way. Did he really use a staple gun?

Ivan was handing them each a pamphlet. "Here's what you need to know," he explained. "And be sure your parents read it. When you're ready, just give me a call."

As she took the pamphlet, Maya explained, "We don't want piercings or tattoos."

"Not yet," added Carolyn, surprised at herself for saying it.

An intercom buzzer rang. "My ten-thirty tongue piercing is here," he said, dismissing them. "New York University is back in session."

Maya moved toward the door. "Okay. So, thanks."

As Maya followed Serge out of the room, she wondered if Joy was right. Maybe she should find another subject for her project.

Two girls passed them on the way into Ivan's operating room.

"Thanks for coming with me," Maya heard the taller girl tell the shorter one. Her voice was shaking. She's really nervous, thought Maya. So why is she doing it? What will it feel like? Will she have trouble talking after? Will food get caught in the stud? Will her tongue get infected, like Shana's belly button?

"Wow!" exclaimed Joy when they were back on the street. "It was way too weird in there."

"That girl's getting her tongue pierced right now," observed Maya. She suddenly realized that she wished she was there photographing the piercing. Even if it did give her the creeps.

"Let's get something to drink," suggested Joy.

Maya spotted a sidewalk café on the corner, and they headed for it.

From an open apartment window, Carolyn heard jazzy trills from someone practicing the trumpet. Looking around at the shops and people — all kinds of people — strolling on the sidewalk, sent a little thrill up Carolyn's spine. New York City. She lived in New York City.

Joy put an arm around Maya's shoulder as they crossed the street. "Don't worry. You'll come up with another idea."

Maya turned to her. "I don't want another idea," she said. "I want to do this one."

Carolyn caught up with them. "You're going to ask Ivan if you can photograph in there?" she asked, surprised.

"Just because it gives me the creeps doesn't mean I don't want to do it," explained Maya, trying to sound brave. "It makes it even more interesting to me." They'd reached the café. "I just have to get Ivan to cooperate. And one of his clients."

They sat at a small table outdoors. "You'd take pictures *while* they're being pierced?" Carolyn asked. "Really?"

Maya nodded.

The waiter came over and took their order for drinks.

"You don't have to go with me, Joy," said Maya. She looked across at Carolyn. "You, either. I can always get Shana to come. Or maybe I'll just go on my own. Serge will be there."

"I *want* to go," protested Carolyn. "I want to see it, too." And I don't want to be afraid of anything, she thought. I want to be the way I was before my mother died. Before 9/11. Before I moved to New York City. Before I lived alone with my dad.

Maya beamed at her. "Okay, Carolyn! It'll be good. You'll see."

Joy looked at the two of them. *School chums*, as Wren would say. Agreeing on everything. She felt like the odd girl out. Just the way she did with the snotty girls in her school. "I'll go, too," she announced. "Maybe I'll have my tongue pierced so you have something to photograph."

Carolyn's eyes widened. "Really?"

"No!" Maya and Joy laughed in unison.

The waiter, who'd just come up to the table with their drinks, hesitated. The girls — realizing that he thought Joy and Maya were saying no to him — laughed even harder.

"We didn't mean you," croaked Maya.

Sneering at the giggling girls, the waiter left the tray of drinks in the middle of the table for them to help themselves.

Suddenly, Serge appeared and pulled up a chair. "I come out for a break and I see you," he announced happily. "Did you like my place of work?"

Maya said she did and that she definitely wanted to photograph someone being pierced at Zeus. Serge said she should call Ivan and wrote down his phone number for her. He looked from Carolyn to Maya. "What do you do for photography class?"

"Nothing yet," admitted Joy.

"I have an idea for mine," Carolyn said. She told them all about Ivy — or as much as she already knew about her.

"That's a great idea for you," commented Maya. "Especially because you love animals so much."

"Ivy's band is performing at a street fair right on Columbus Avenue," Carolyn concluded. "Next Sunday."

"We should all go," suggested Maya.

"Sunday is my day off," announced Serge. "I like the drums."

I guess he's coming, too, thought Maya with surprise.

Joy did a quick calendar calculation in her head. Next Sunday she was scheduled to be back at her dad's. She hadn't asked him yet if she could live full-time at her mom's. I can always come uptown to the fair, she thought. But it would be so great to just walk across the park and be there. I'll go to his office after school on Monday. But what will I say to him? How can I ask him so he has to say yes? She remembered how Carolyn's father was going to send her back to Wyoming at the end of last summer. And how she and Maya had helped Carolyn convince him to let her stay in New York. Maya could be smart about psychological stuff. Maybe, when Serge left, she'd ask Maya and Carolyn for advice. Maybe.

"So I'm staying at Maya's house for ten days," Carolyn was telling Serge. "While my dad is at this convention in Thailand."

Joy snapped out of her own thoughts and back into the conversation. "You are?" she said, surprised.

Carolyn nodded. "It'll be so great. We can go to school together. And Josie's going to do my whole astrological chart while I'm there." She turned to Serge. "When's your birthday? Maya can tell you what your sign is."

Joy didn't listen to Serge's answer. She didn't care about Serge's sign. She didn't know much about astrology. It was another thing that Carolyn and Maya had in common. One more way that she was the odd girl out.

"The longer you put off calling Ivan, the harder it will be to do it," Carolyn told Maya after school on Wednesday. Carolyn pulled her toward the doorway of a stationery store and took the cell phone out of her pocket. "You should call him right now! Use my dad's phone."

"Okay, okay," agreed Maya. "I'll do it." She took the paper with Ivan's number out of her bag and dialed. "What if he isn't there?" she whispered. "What if Wren answers?"

"Say you'll call back later," advised Carolyn.

But Ivan was there. "I thought you were the one who'd get a piercing first," he said.

Maya told him she wasn't calling about getting pierced. Then she explained about the photo workshop and how she wanted to take pictures of a piercing.

"You can't just come in here and take pictures," he said. "That could freak out a client."

"I thought maybe you could ask someone for me," she explained. "When they make an appointment."

It was a cool day, but Maya's palms were sweaty. Why did Ivan make her so nervous?

"Okay," he finally agreed. "I'll ask someone I think might go for it. But it'll have to be someone who books in advance. You interested in any special part of the body?"

Maya remembered the girl from New York University. "A tongue. That'd be great."

"A tongue? Sure," he said. "I get lots of those. I'll call you."

"Thank you," she said, surprised and relieved that it had been so easy.

"No problem. My daughters get some pretty way-out homework, and they're only in the second grade."

When Maya handed Carolyn back the phone she announced, "He's got kids. Girls in the second grade. I guess they're twins."

"With identical tattoos and piercings," said Carolyn.

Maya laughed. "I wonder what they do on Take Your Daughter to Work Day?"

Joy walked through the crush of pedestrians on Wall Street into her father's office building. She stood in line to have her bag searched. It was, Joy suddenly realized, the first time she'd been to her father's office since the terrorist attacks on the World Trade Center. That was over a year ago and before the new security measures — like checking bags.

As the elevator rose up through the center of the building to the forty-first floor, ripples of nausea and fear ran through her. She'd always been a little afraid of being in tall buildings. But now — after watching the Twin Towers fall — she was terrified.

She got off the elevator and went into the offices of Cohen and Lieberman Financial Services.

The receptionist looked up, smiling. "May I help you?"

"I'm here to see my father," Joy answered. "Ted Cohen."

"Oh," said the receptionist with surprise. "I thought he only had the little boy. You can go back, Miss Cohen. You know where he is?"

Joy nodded.

Her father was standing at his desk, talking into a telephone headset. He was, she could see by his expression, surprised to see her. He motioned for her to sit down. She sat and waited while he counseled a client about losses in the stock market. She looked at the gallery of framed photos on a bookshelf. Her father and Sue's wedding picture. Three pictures of Jake. And an old school picture of her, scowling at the camera. It was taken at least three years ago. She hated that picture.

Her father, finally finished with the call, was now looking at the flickering numbers on his computer monitor. "Business is in the toilet," he mumbled to himself.

She cleared her throat to remind him that she was there.

He finally looked at her. "Sorry, honey. I wasn't

expecting you." He looked down at his calendar. "Should I have been?"

"No."

He glanced nervously at the flashing numbers on the monitor again. "Is everything all right, Joy?"

She shifted in the chair. "Dad, I need you to do something for me," she began. "It's about school."

"I paid my half of your tuition," he said. "If there's anything missing, it's your mother's —"

"It's not about the tuition," Joy said, interrupting him.

The phone rang. He flicked on the intercom and told the receptionist to hold his calls, then turned back to Joy. Waiting.

"What I need," she continued, determined not to stop until she'd gotten it all out, "is more time to do my schoolwork. I want to live uptown full-time, at least for the school year. My school's, like, only three blocks from Mom's. Besides, all my friends are uptown. And I'm sick of going back and forth. It's hard to keep worrying about where my stuff is. So I want to stay at Mom's. Uptown."

"Was this your mother's idea?" he asked.

"No," protested Joy. "It's all my idea."

"And who's going to be there for you after school?" he asked. "Your mother is a workaholic. She has to travel for that company of hers."

Joy glared at him. Why couldn't her parents understand that she didn't want to hear their criticisms of each other? That she wasn't taking sides and never would.

"I know, I'm a workaholic, too," he admitted. He leaned toward her. "But at least when you're with me, Sue and Jake are there. You have a real family."

No, she wanted to say again. But she didn't. I'm not here to argue with him, she reminded herself. I'm here to get what I want.

"I'll get better grades if I don't have to waste time on the subway," she pleaded. "And I'll get to see my friends more. You're always nagging me to be more social."

"Won't you miss your little brother?"

No, she thought. "I'll stay with you guys when Mom's out of town," she offered. "And weekends, sometimes."

"I'll have to ask Sue about this," he said, distracted again by the ringing phone.

She was about to protest that Sue shouldn't have anything to do with it, when the receptionist burst into the room. "Mr. Cohen," she said. "The president of Chazen Smith is on the line. He says it's urgent. I thought you'd want to know."

"Thank you, Rachel," he said as he pulled up the phone headset. He nodded at Joy. "I have to take this. It's confidential. Wait in reception." He motioned for her to follow Rachel out of the room.

When they reached the reception area, Joy opened the door to the outside hall. "Tell my father I had to leave," she said. Heading toward the elevator she thought, Maybe I just won't show up on change-over day. Dad and Sue won't even notice — unless they need a baby-sitter. They should get a new sitter anyway — one who *likes* babies and knows about earaches.

As she was waiting for the elevator, her father came running out of the office. "Joy. Don't go."

She turned to face him. "I just think I should be able to live where I want," she said sharply. "I'm not a kid anymore."

He stopped in front of her and put his hands on her shoulders. "Okay. We can try it for a month," he said. "But I want to have dinner with you every week. Okay?"

"Just the two of us?" she asked.

"Sure," he said. "Why not? But sometimes it should be the whole family. Otherwise, you won't see Jake and your stepmother." As the elevator doors opened, he gave her a quick peck on the cheek and turned to go back to his office.

When Joy was safely on the street, she pumped a fist and whispered, "Yes!" But walking away from the building her mood darkened. Why had her father agreed so quickly? Doesn't he even care if I live with him? she wondered. Is he glad to have me out of the way so he can be alone with his new family all the time — not just on alternate weeks? He said he'd have dinner with me. Just the two of us. But will he be wishing he was with Sue and Jake instead?

Her uncle Brett used to see her one evening a

week. "Rain or shine, once a week you're mine," he used to say. When he was sick with AIDS, all they could do was sit and watch an old movie together and eat take-out. Even then, Uncle Brett always seemed more interested in her than her own parents. Her eyes filled with tears. She missed him.

Columbus Avenue

The ringing telephone woke Joy. She picked it up and glanced at the clock. Ten o'clock.

It was Jay-Cee. Joy stretched herself awake. This morning she was taking more photos for Jay-Cee's modeling portfolio. Maya and Carolyn were going to be there.

"Where am I meeting you?" Jay-Cee asked. "Inside the Plaza Hotel or in front of it?"

"Meet me out front, near the fountain," Joy told her. "The Plaza doesn't like people hanging out in their lobby who aren't staying there."

"I have these really cool boots for today," Jay-Cee announced enthusiastically. "And I'm bringing another outfit. Modeling agencies want to see how you look in different clothes."

Does she ever think about anything but how good she looks and who's noticing? wondered Joy. They were meeting at eleven. She'd better get a move on.

An hour later, Joy crossed Fifth Avenue at 60th Street. The castlelike Plaza Hotel loomed up in front of her, its cream-colored stone glowing in the sunlight. I was right, she thought, the Plaza will be a good backdrop. And Central Park is right across the street. We can shoot pictures there, too. Maybe do some with a horse and buggy.

Joy spotted Jay-Cee and Maya sitting at the edge of the fountain. She checked out Jay-Cee's outfit. A short animal-print skirt, tube top, and short black velvet jacket. High, thin-heeled boots. Her crossed legs showed off fishnet stockings. Maya was in camouflage cargo pants, a black T-shirt, and a short brown jacket. Joy was sure Maya had gotten that jacket from her mother's secondhand clothing store, Remember Me. Maya and I sort of dress alike now, she thought.

Two hands suddenly grabbed Joy from behind. Carolyn wheeled in front of her, flushed and grinning.

"Maya let me use her Rollerblades," Carolyn announced excitedly. "I never did it before. I love it!" She rolled off for another turn around the fountain.

Joy took pictures of Jay-Cee near the fountain, in front of the Plaza, and beside a horse-drawn carriage. Maya thought they should take some shots of Jay-Cee *in* the carriage and told the buggy driver that it would be good for business.

"Okay by me," he said. "Business has been lousy lately."

Jay-Cee climbed in. A couple of tourists stopped to watch. "Is this for a magazine?" the woman asked Joy.

"Not exactly," she answered.

"But you might see me in a magazine *someday*," bragged Jay-Cee.

While Joy shot, Carolyn stood in front of the horse, a tawny Belgian. She looked into the mare's liquid, bright eyes and thought about her own horse, Tailgate. The two weeks home had been wonderful. She'd ridden Tailgate every day, helped out on the ranch, hunted rabbits with her grandfather, and had an overnight trek with her best friend, Mandy.

Carolyn put a hand on the carriage horse's neck. Do you like being a carriage horse? she silently asked. Do you like living in New York City? She felt the answer through the animal's pulse and the look in her eye. This was a healthy, happy horse.

Someone poked her shoulder, snapping her back into the world of humans. It was Jay-Cee. "I need my stuff. I'm going to change."

The tourist couple was climbing into the buggy, and Carolyn moved away from the horse. "Where are you going to change?" she asked Jay-Cee as she handed off the backpack.

"In the hotel," answered Jay-Cee, matter-of-factly.

"The Plaza is pretty swanky," observed Maya. "They might not let you —"

"I can handle it," Jay-Cee assured her. She turned to Joy. "I need you to come with me, though. We're going to pretend we're staying there. Put on an attitude, girl."

As they ascended the Plaza steps, Jay-Cee turned to Joy and spoke in a voice the doorman could overhear. "Did my mother say to meet her in the lobby or the room? Do you remember?"

"The room," Joy answered without missing a beat.

The doorman nodded respectfully to them as they walked in.

Jay-Cee looked around at the elegant furniture, palm trees, and flower arrangements.

Joy had been in the Plaza before. Uncle Brett and his partner had brought her there for high tea on her tenth birthday. Now that she was inside, she remembered the location of the rest rooms. "Follow me," she whispered.

While Jay-Cee changed in the stall, Joy sat in an easy chair near the mirrors. She glanced at her reflection. Was her top too tight? A guy on the subway had definitely ogled her breasts. It gave her the creeps. She remembered how she used to hide her figure under baggy clothes. Maybe sometimes baggy wasn't such a bad idea.

Jay-Cee came out of the stall in a long, gauzy red skirt and a hot-pink tank top. The net stockings were off and the boots were replaced with spike-heeled gold sandals. She took out her makeup bag and leaned toward the mirror.

"I like your skirt," commented Joy. "Is it from Remember Me?"

"The fabric's from there," answered Jay-Cee. "I repair clothes for Maya's mom. She pays me with fabric and lets me make stuff on her machine." Jay-Cee's mirrored reflection smiled at Joy. "I'm going to make a skirt for you. To thank you for doing all this."

"You made that skirt?" asked Joy, surprised.

Jay-Cee nodded. "I make most of my own clothes. Design them, too. I'm going to be a clothing designer."

"I thought you wanted to be a model."

"Only to make money for design school and to start up my own business." She drew a black line on her lower eyelid. "You don't think that I'm planning on being some kind of high-fashion model, do you?"

Joy was confused. "I thought that's why we were doing this. Taking pictures for your portfolio."

Jay-Cee pointed the eyeliner at her. "Girl, I have a better grip on what's possible than that! I'm going to try for catalog work and runway jobs in stores. And only thanks to you, for taking these pictures." She handed Joy a lipstick. "You should use this. It would look good on you."

As Joy applied Jay-Cee's bright red lipstick, she thought about her. Jay-Cee made her own clothes. She was going to put herself through college. She wanted to run her own business. There was way more to Jay-Cee than makeup and long fingernails, she thought.

Jay-Cee straightened up. "I'm ready."

"That doorman's going to be surprised when he sees you in a whole other outfit," commented Joy.

Joy pushed the rest room door open for her. "He'll just think I changed in my mother's room," Jay-Cee said as she strode out.

Laughing, Joy followed her.

Jay-Cee in front of the Plaza, red skirt blowing up around her knees. Click.

Jay-Cee by the fountain. From another angle. From farther away. Click. Click. Click.

Then Maya was beside Joy, saying, "We have to go soon. Serge is meeting us at Seventy-Second Street in half an hour. It'll take us that long to get there."

Joy took one more shot and turned off her camera.

Carolyn spun around in front of them.

"Are you sure this is the first day you've skated, girl?" asked Jay-Cee.

"You can keep them on in the park, if you want," offered Maya.

Carolyn spun again and shouted, "Yes."

Once they were in the park, she skated ahead of the walkers. On a flat stretch now, she turned and bladed backward. She wished her father would let her have Rollerblades.

Serge was waiting for them in Strawberry Fields, the memorial park to John Lennon. Carolyn's mom and dad had both loved Beatles music. This part of Central Park was one of the first places Carolyn and her father had visited when they first moved to New York.

To reach Serge, Carolyn skated around the large circle in the pavement with IMAGINE written in the center. Visitors had laid single flowers on it. A man strummed the Beatles tune "Yesterday" on a guitar. Carolyn remembered listening to it with her mother the week before she died.

"I saw the street fair," Serge announced to the girls. "It is very cool and rocking."

Joy and Carolyn exchanged a grin. "Our chum's English is improving fast," Joy whispered.

Carolyn took the skates off and gave them back to Maya. The fair was in her neighborhood. She didn't want to bump into her dad with them on.

For the fair, Columbus Avenue was closed to traffic. The five of them wandered uptown in the middle of the wide road. It was mobbed with people but no one was rushing. Booth tents selling jewelry, candles, leather bags, hand-painted T-shirts, wooden-framed mirrors, and more things than Carolyn could keep track of lined both sides of the street. There were food booths, too. And a stage. A rapper with a DJ backup was performing. *Serge is right,* she thought. *This fair is cool and rocking.*

They all bought lunch. Joy, Jay-Cee, and Serge had Italian sausages. Maya and Carolyn got vegetable curry and samosas from an Indian food stand. They sat on the curb to eat and listen to the rapper while they waited for the Big Bang Band. It was hard to see with the passersby and the crowd standing in front of the stage.

When Carolyn finished eating, she took out her camera and put in a new roll of film. Maya leaned toward her and pointed at the stage. "Is that woman with the short hair Ivy?"

Carolyn looked up. The rapper and DJ had left the stage. Ivy was walking on. She carried a set of bongo drums in one hand and wheeled a metal frame covered in hanging pots and pans with the other. Her short hair was streaked with green and spiked. She had on black jeans, a purple tank top, and a denim jacket. Two other women were on the stage. One was setting up an electric keyboard. The other was tuning a violin.

"That's her," said Carolyn.

"You should photograph her setting up," suggested Joy.

Carolyn's stomach churned over her lunch. How could she go up there and start taking photographs in front of everyone?

Maya gave her a little push. "Go," she ordered. "Do it."

"Remember what Beth said," added Joy. "Get her from lots of angles."

"And don't be afraid to get close," added Maya.

Carolyn went toward the stage. When she started shooting, she stopped being nervous.

Ivy tightening her bongo drum. Click.

Ivy adding bells to the rack of silver and black pots and pans. Click.

By the time the Big Bang Band started playing, Ivy had taken off her jacket and Carolyn was on her second roll of film.

Ivy banging on the pots with a drumstick and her fist. Click.

The band's sound was loud and pulsing. It had a steady beat and a rhythm that became more complex as it speeded up. The violin whined and soared. It was intense. Carolyn had never heard music like that before. By the second number, she began taking pictures to the beat. *Click. Click. Click-click-click.*

Close-up shot of Ivy kicking the pans in martial-arts moves. Click.

Carolyn turned to face the audience.

Wide-angle shot of the crowd. Click.

When the Big Bang Band finished their set, their sound still swirled and pounded in her head. Maya and the others wove through the crowd toward her.

Ivy wheeled her pots-and-pans instrument to the edge of the stage. Serge reached up to help her lift it down, but she motioned him away. "If a musician can't carry her own instrument," she told him, "she shouldn't be playing it."

"Tell that to Horowitz," muttered Joy.

Carolyn hoped that Ivy hadn't heard Joy's sarcastic comment.

"Who?" asked Jay-Cee.

"Horowitz was Russian," Serge announced proudly.

"And a famous pianist," added Joy.

"Well, he couldn't carry *his* instrument," said Jay-Cee.

Joy put a friendly arm around her shoulder. "Exactly my point."

Ivy came up to Carolyn. "How'd you like it?"

"Great," said Carolyn enthusiastically. "It was — ah — pretty unusual. But I liked it."

"I didn't mean our sound," explained Ivy. "I meant how did you like doing *your* thing. You know, photographing it."

"It was fun," she answered, realizing, as she said it, that it *had* been fun.

"I'd like to see those pictures. I might be able to use some for publicity. Of course I'd give you credit."

"I'll have a set made for you," Carolyn offered.

Ivy dug into her jeans' pocket and handed Carolyn a card. "Now you don't have to hang around waiting for me to walk dogs." She turned and ran back to the stage for the rest of her instruments.

Maya pulled on Carolyn's arm. "Let's go drop off your pictures," she suggested. "You can get them back today if we do it now."

That evening, Carolyn put the two envelopes of photographs and Ivy's card in the top drawer of her bureau. She didn't want to leave them out where her father might see them. He would ask too many questions. She'd explain about Ivy and the photography project another time. As she was coming into the kitchen to help with dinner, the phone rang. It wasn't the regular phone, she noticed, but her father's cell phone. She opened a cabinet and took out a box of rice and the measuring cup.

He answered his phone with his usual "This is Donald Kuhlberg."

Carolyn turned on the faucet to measure out water for the rice.

"Maya? Are you looking for Maya Johnson?" her father was saying.

Carolyn stopped mid-action. Why was someone calling Maya on her father's phone?

"Well, Mr. Kaminsky, you have the wrong number," he said.

Who is Mr. Kaminsky? wondered Carolyn.

Her father closed the phone and turned to her. "Who is Ivan Kaminsky? Do you know a place called Zeus? And why did this Ivan have my phone number?"

No way was she telling her father about the piercing parlor. It would only upset him and make trouble for her. So she only answered his last question. "I don't know, Dad."

That was the truth. She didn't know why Ivan had called her father's cell phone.

"Do your friends use my phone?" he asked. "When you have it?"

"I guess, once in a while," she answered. "Not Joy. She has her own. But maybe Maya. To call home."

"Or to call Ivan at Zeus," her father said. "That's it. He must have had my number in his call log because she called him on my phone. He thought it was her number."

"Maybe Zeus is where Maya has her hair cut," added Carolyn. It wasn't a lie. Not exactly.

"Maybe," he agreed.

She turned back to making the rice.

*   *   *

"Read me another story," Piper begged Maya. "You didn't read me one last night, so you *owe* me."

Maya tapped her little sister's nose. "You owe me a kiss and hug good night."

Piper hugged her big sister and whispered in her ear, "Please read me another Frog and Toad. Please, please, please."

"If you promise to close your eyes while I'm reading," Maya bargained. She settled Piper back on the pillow and opened the book. What she really wanted to do was tell Carolyn and Joy the news. Ivan had called. She had an appointment to photograph a guy named Alex. He was a friend of Serge's who was having his tongue pierced on Saturday morning, and he'd agreed to be photographed.

Sue folded Joy's denim jacket. "This will always be your room, Joy," she said, handing it to her.

Joy put the jacket in her old camp trunk.

Sue took a black linen shirt and pants set from the closet. It was oversized — one of the many outfits Joy used to hide in. "I guess you won't be taking this," she said, dropping it on the bed. "That's the way the old Joy dressed. You look so much better in clothes that fit." Glancing around the room, she added, "Do you mind if I put a treadmill in here?"

Joy thought, She can't wait to get rid of me, and told her, "Do whatever you want."

"I hate that you're leaving us," Sue said.

Right, thought Joy. Her cell phone rang. She opened it, saw the call was from Maya, and said, "Hi."

Maya told her about the piercing appointment at Zeus.

Joy sat on the edge of the bed. Sue was still there, listening, Joy knew, to every word. The last thing she wanted was for Sue to know her business.

"Do you still want to go with me?" Maya asked.

"Sure I do. It'll be fun. Well, maybe not *fun* fun. But it will be interesting."

"It won't creep you out too much?" asked Maya.

It will creep me out in a *major* way, thought Joy. But I won't tell Maya that. Carolyn will go for sure. I don't want to be left out. "No, really, I'd love to go," she told Maya. "I'm there."

When Joy hung up, Sue asked, "Who was that?"

"Just a friend," answered Joy.

Sue sat on the bed beside her. "Do you know what I think?" she said conspiratorially. "I think that it was a boy and that he lives uptown and that's why you want to live with your mom all the time. Tell me I'm wrong."

Joy just smiled. She wasn't going to give Sue the satisfaction of an answer. Let her think what she wanted.

Her father came into the room with Jake. "How's it going in here?" he asked. "Need any help from the guys?"

"I think Joy has her own guy," announced Sue. "Now that she has her new look." Sue held up the linen outfit again. "This was not the way to interest boys." She grinned at Joy. "You finally followed my advice."

You had *nothing* to do with my makeover, thought Joy. *Nothing.*

"Well, Joy looks like a girl who would be asked on dates, doesn't she?" her father said. "I'm proud of you, Joy."

Proud of how I dress? thought Joy. Proud of how I do my hair? People are so caught up in looks. I'm the same person I was when my hair was hanging in my face and I wore baggy clothes and weighed a little more. Why should I be treated differently now? She remembered the guy who sold incense on the street. Before she'd changed her look, he had called her a fat cow. After, he had whistled and flirted. Before, no one seemed to notice her, unless it was to criticize. After, people told her how good she looked. An idea flashed in her head. She suddenly knew what she wanted to do for her photography project. She'd need Maya's and Carolyn's help. And maybe Jay-Cee's. Yes. Jay-Cee would be perfect.

Sue and her father were fussing over Jake, encouraging him to take his first steps. "Do it for your sister, before she goes," her father was saying.

Joy took the baggy outfit Sue had left on the bed and put it in her trunk. She was taking it with her after all. She might need it.

Zeus

Carolyn tugged on Maya's sleeve and pointed to a guy walking into Zeus ahead of them. "Maybe that's Alex," she whispered to Maya.

The boy, seeing the three girls behind him, held the door open.

Carolyn checked him out as she walked past him. He was an average-sized teenager with short dreadlocks, a big smile, and just one piercing that she could see — on his ear.

The guy didn't look at her, though. His attention was on Wren, who was arranging jewelry in the counter-display case. "Hi, Wren," he called out.

Wren barely glanced his way. "Yeah. Hi. Serge is in the back."

The boy leaned over the counter so she'd have to look at him. "I'm not here to see Serge. I have an appointment with Ivan. I'm getting my tongue pierced."

Carolyn elbowed Maya. She was right.

"The tongue, Alex?" Wren said. "Great." She finally looked over at him.

Alex beamed. "Yeah."

He really likes Wren, thought Maya. Is he having his tongue pierced to impress her?

"You going to hold my hand, Wren?" Alex asked. "While he does it?"

Wren looked around at the girls. "You don't need me to hold your hand. You've got the chick clique here."

"We didn't come with him," Carolyn told her.

Maya held up her camera. "I'm the photographer," she said to Alex. "Ivan said it would be okay with you."

Serge came out from the back of the store and stood beside Maya. "Ivan is ready for Alex," he announced.

"Good luck," Wren told Alex.

Carolyn thought Wren's way of saying, "Good luck," was sarcastic. Like when Joy said, "Have a nice day."

"And Alex, come tell me all about it right after," Wren added. "Because you won't be talking so good for the next few days."

Alex's eyes widened. "Really?"

Serge slapped Alex on the back. "It is not so bad. Come on." He turned to Joy and Carolyn. "Ivan said Maya alone can watch."

Carolyn was disappointed.

Joy was relieved. "We'll wait out here," she offered.

Alex glanced over his shoulder. Carolyn saw the worry in his eyes. "Good luck, Alex," she said. And she meant it.

Maya followed Alex into Ivan's studio. First, Ivan asked him for his signed forms and the payment.

Then he carefully explained how he should take care of his tongue after the piercing. *Click.*

Ivan showing Alex the barbell he'll put in his tongue. Click.

Ivan slipping on surgical gloves. Click.

Alex rinsing with Listerine. Click.

Alex's tongue held out by a clamp. Click.

Maya's heartbeat sped up. Keep taking pictures, she told herself.

Drool leaking out of the sides of Alex's mouth. Click.

"Take a long deep breath, Alex," Ivan instructed. "I'm going to pierce it on the exhale."

Alex took a deep breath and let it go.

The needle going through the tongue. Click.

Ivan screwing in the barbell. Click.

"You're done," Ivan announced as he removed the clamp from Alex's tongue.

"You already did it?" Alex asked, confused.

"You got a problem with that?" teased Ivan.

Alex moved his tongue around in his mouth and touched the barbell to his upper lip. "It's okay," he said, surprised. "It feels okay."

"That's the way it's supposed to be," Ivan told him. "Just be sure you follow all the directions for keeping it clean."

Ivan handing Alex a copy of after-care instructions. Click.

"Wren has the products you need," Ivan continued. "Come by next Saturday, and I'll take a look at it."

Serge was waiting outside the operating room.

"Hey, man, that wasn't so bad," Alex bragged. He stuck out his tongue.

Carolyn and Joy came over to see.

Alex's pierced tongue. Click.

"Alex, can I call you in a few days to see how it's going?" Maya asked.

"Sure," he agreed.

He wrote down his phone number for Maya.

"I have all this stuff here for you," Wren called to him. "Come over here and let me see what Ivan did to you."

The girls said good-bye and left.

Maya took a deep breath of the crisp fall air. She felt light-headed and happy. I did it, she thought. She told Joy and Carolyn, "I think I got some good shots."

They walked down the street. "Wren's treating Alex nicer because he had it done," commented Carolyn.

"I think she was jealous that he gave his phone number to Maya," said Joy.

"And I think he had his tongue pierced to impress Wren," added Maya.

"Ah, love," cooed Carolyn. "Ain't it grand?"

"Ain't it grand?" mimicked Joy. "Where did you get that?"

"It's something my grandfather is always saying," Carolyn answered.

"Deep," Joy commented.

Carolyn poked Maya in the arm. "Hey. Tell us about the piercing."

Joy tuned out Maya's description of Alex's tongue piercing. She needed to talk to Carolyn and Maya about her project, and she wanted to do it before the workshop. But she was nervous. What if they didn't like her idea? She checked her watch. "You want to get something for lunch before we go to the workshop? We have time."

"How about *something* like pizza?" suggested Carolyn.

"Pizza," teased Joy. "Ain't it grand?"

When they were sitting in a booth, each with a slice and soda, Joy told them she had an idea for her photography project. "I want to show that people are treated differently depending on how they dress and act," she began.

"In photographs?" asked Carolyn, confused. "How?"

"I'll have two girls dressed sloppily," she began. "Like losers —"

Like you used to dress, thought Maya.

"Like I used to dress," continued Joy, repeating Maya's thought. "So these two girls walk down the street, go to a café, and order something."

"Candid camera," put in Carolyn.

"That's right," agreed Joy. "I'll secretly take pictures. My photographs will show how they're treated. You know, by the waiter. The expression on his face, that sort of thing."

"Then you'll have the same two girls go back all dressed up and looking good," said Maya. "And shoot more pictures. Am I right?"

"You got it," Joy exclaimed, pleased that Maya understood her idea.

Maya looked at Carolyn. "Now I just wonder who those two girls are going to be?"

"Actually," Joy told Maya, "I was hoping you'd do camera with me. You have that real good telephoto lens." She looked at Carolyn. "I'd like you and Jay-Cee to be the actors."

"Jay-Cee will love that," commented Maya.

"I might call it, 'You Can't Judge a Book by Its Cover,'" said Joy. "I mean if it works out. Do you think that the title's too old-fashioned?"

"That's what I like about it," Carolyn told her.

"Ain't it grand?!" laughed Maya.

Sunday afternoon, Carolyn and Maya did their homework together. Maya's room was on the top floor of the Johnsons' four-story brownstone. While Maya finished her history homework, Carolyn sat at the window, looking out. Two of Maya's sisters were playing hopscotch with their friends on the sidewalk. Josie was down the street, talking to a neighbor.

Maya closed her notebook. "Done," she said.

"Time to call Alex," Carolyn reminded her.

As Maya was dialing, Carolyn saw two girls Rollerblading down the block. "I think Shana and Delores are coming here," she told Maya.

Maya remembered a vague plan to go Roller-blading with Shana and Delores if the weather was nice. Sunlight streamed in through her window. The weather was nice.

"Ell-o," said the voice on the other end of the phone.

"Alex?" said Maya.

"Ess. Dis is Alec."

"Are you okay?" Maya asked as she motioned Carolyn to come listen on the phone with her.

"Caan alk oo-o goo-d."

"Ivan said your tongue would be swollen," Maya reminded him. "Are you sucking on ice the way he said?"

"I ammm. Erry hour."

Carolyn and Maya exchanged a look. Alex sounded really bad.

"Can you eat anything?" asked Carolyn.

"Milk shaakes. Uice."

"You doing all the stuff you're supposed to do so it doesn't get infected?" asked Maya.

"Ess."

Maya wondered if she should take pictures of his swollen tongue. Just the thought of it made her stomach turn over. Instead she said, "See you next Saturday."

"O-ay. Gaa-uh go uck ice. Byye."

"Take care of yourself," Maya said before she hung up.

Piper ran into the room. "Shana's here! Shana's

here!" she shouted. Shana and Delores were right behind her, their blades over their shoulders.

When Shana noticed Carolyn, she looked away
without acknowledging her.

She *really* doesn't like me, Carolyn thought.

As if to cover up for Shana's rudeness, Delores
asked Carolyn, "So what's up?"

"Maya just called this guy Alex," Carolyn answered. "He had his tongue pierced yesterday morning and Maya took pictures." She was *not* going to let
Shana intimidate her.

Delores sat on the bed. "You took pictures, M?
Oh, gross."

"He was sort of a sweet guy," said Carolyn. "But
he was really scared."

"White, I suppose," said Shana.

"No, he wasn't," Carolyn answered.

"Besides, what difference does that make,
Shana?" added Maya.

"Tongues can be hard," Delores remarked. "My
uncle had his pierced and it got oh-so-swollen."

"That's what happened to Alex," said Carolyn, recovering from Shana's rudeness. "We were afraid it
would get infected, like Shana's belly button did."

Shana walked toward Carolyn at the window, her
hands on her hips. "Like Shana's *what*?" she asked.

Carolyn moved away from the open window.
But Shana wasn't coming toward her anymore. She'd
turned to Maya. "You telling people my personal business?"

"Sorry," said Maya. "I didn't think it was a secret. You told everybody."

"Not *everybody*," Shana shot back with a glance in Carolyn's direction.

Shana is such a typical Scorpio, thought Maya. Possessive and jealous. But she didn't say that to Shana. She tried to remember her good qualities. Loyal and determined. In second grade, when the most popular girls decided that Maya was stuck-up and excluded her, Shana defended her and remained her friend. By the time Maya was back in the girl pack, she and Shana were best friends.

"I said I was sorry, Shana," Maya said. "I mean it."

"Me, too," Shana replied softly.

Shana didn't say she was sorry to me, thought Carolyn.

"Let's just put it in gear and go blading," said Delores. "That's the plan, isn't it?"

"Carolyn doesn't have skates," said Maya.

"That's okay," put in Carolyn. "I'm supposed to be home pretty soon." She didn't want to spend any more time with Shana than she had to, anyway. "You guys go."

The phone in Maya's room rang. It was Joy.

"I talked to Jay-Cee," she told Maya. "You were right. She'll work on my project. Are you free on Friday? Maybe we can use Carolyn's apartment for changing clothes. It's right around the corner from the café where I want to do the shoot. Do you think her dad will let us?"

"You can ask her," Maya told her. "She's right here." She handed Carolyn the phone. Maya knew Shana was pouting, so she avoided looking at her.

Carolyn and Joy talked about the shoot. Friday after school would be perfect, Carolyn thought. Her father would be at the museum. She'd just tell him that Maya and Joy were coming over to work on a project. She was sure he'd say yes. Every week, it seemed, she was getting more and more privileges. Soon she'd ask him for Rollerblades again.

She asked Joy what she should wear. "Sloppy, so you don't look too pretty," Joy explained. "And cover your hair."

"What about when I'm looking nice? Should I wear a dress, or what?" Carolyn asked.

"Jay-Cee's going to take care of that," Joy told her. "And she wants to know what size shoe you wear."

"Eight," answered Carolyn, as she imagined herself in one of the outfits Jay-Cee had worn for her portfolio shots. This was going to be fun.

"Are we waiting until it's dark to go blading?" Shana asked.

Sarcasm rules, thought Carolyn.

Joy followed the maître d' to a table in the center of the restaurant. Her father was already there. It was, she knew, his favorite midtown restaurant. He stood as she approached. "You're here," he said with a kiss to her cheek. "And you look lovely."

She felt lovely, in black satin pants and a bronze

silk shirt she'd bought from Maya's mother's second-hand clothing store. The maître d' pulled out a chair for her and she sat.

"That blouse looks terrific on you. Is it new?"

"Sort of," she answered. She wondered what her father would think if she told him it was secondhand and only cost twelve dollars. Sue spent hundreds of dollars for an outfit. I used to, too, thought Joy.

After they studied the menu and talked about what they'd order, her father told Joy all the cute things that Jake was doing. Things he thought were cute, anyway. He leaned forward and looked a little sad. "You know, I think he misses you."

Joy knew her father wanted her to talk about Jake and be enthusiastic about his every burp. To be courteous, she asked, "Is he walking yet?"

"Any day," he answered.

She changed the subject by asking how things were at his office.

"They've been better," he answered. A ripple of worry wrinkled his forehead. "But nothing for you to trouble yourself about. These things always turn around." He signaled for the waiter, and they placed their order. When the waiter was gone, he said, "Tell me how things are with you. School. Your friends. Not having you at home, I'm not keeping up with these things."

"School's okay," she answered. What else could she tell him? "And I like the photography workshop. I'm doing the assignments with Maya and Joy again. The girls I worked with last summer."

"Really?" he said enthusiastically. "What are you all photographing?"

She didn't want to tell him about the piercing parlor. He wouldn't approve, and he'd worry that she was hanging out with the wrong people. The thought of her father — all proper in his suit and tie — walking into Zeus made her smile. My dad can be such a yuppie snob, she thought. She didn't want to try to explain her project, either. She wasn't sure she understood it herself. Carolyn's project seemed like a safe subject.

Joy was describing Ivy's structure of pots and pans when a woman and man came over to their table. The woman beamed at her father. "Ted. Ted Cohen," she gushed. She turned to the man with her. "You know my husband, Randall."

Her father greeted them and gestured toward Joy. "This is my daughter, Joy," he said. "The joy of my life. Joy, this is Geraldine Bourne and her husband, Randall. Geraldine and I are business associates."

Joy smiled at the Bournes and at her father. He had called her "the joy of my life!" He hadn't said that since Jake was born.

Carolyn was supposed to be having dinner with her father, too. Only he wasn't home yet. She was sitting on the couch flipping through *Natural History* magazine when she finally heard his key in the lock.

He seemed surprised to see her there. "You're home early."

She stood up. "You said I should be home by

five o'clock. It's six. I thought you wanted to have dinner early tonight."

"Did I say that?" he asked.

He looked funny to her. Something was different about him. He had on his best sports jacket and new jeans instead of his baggy khakis. That was it. He hardly ever wore jeans. His face was flushed.

"Where were you?" she asked, sounding — she knew — like a parent.

"I — uh — went for a nice walk in the park. It was such a nice day and you were gone." He hesitated. "Just me. By myself. It was really nice."

She laughed. "Dad, you just used 'nice' three times in a row. And you said, 'Just me. By myself.' They mean the same thing. It's redundant. You hate it when I talk like that!"

"Did I do that?" he asked, going into the kitchen area.

She followed him. "Are you okay, Dad?"

"I'm fine." He saw their places set at the counter and breathed in the cooking smells. "You made dinner all by yourself. That's so nice. Thank you."

He said *nice* again, she thought. What's wrong with him?

West 82nd Street

By four o'clock on Friday, Carolyn and Jay-Cee were dressed for the first part of Joy's shoot. Carolyn had on Joy's oversized black blouse, an old skirt that Maya had brought for her, and a pair of run-down loafers.

Maya tucked Carolyn's attention-getting red hair into a frumpy cap.

Jay-Cee had on baggy jeans and an oversized sweatshirt.

Joy checked her out. "The makeup has to go."

Jay-Cee removed her makeup, but left black smudges of eyeliner under her eyes.

Jay-Cee put an arm around Carolyn's shoulder and asked, "How do we look?"

"Great," Joy assured her. "You look really awful."

Carolyn grinned.

"No smiles," added Joy. "And you should slump."

"Don't make eye contact with people," added Maya.

I hope I don't bump into anyone I know, Carolyn thought as they left the apartment.

She didn't.

A few minutes later, the four girls were in position for the shoot.

Jay-Cee and Carolyn waited at the corner for the signal to go.

Joy stood in the bus stop shelter. From there, she had a clear view of the sidewalk leading up to the café and the table she'd told Carolyn and Jay-Cee to take.

Maya was stationed across the street with her telephoto lens.

Joy pointed a finger at her actresses and mouthed, "Go." She looked through the viewfinder.

Two girls walking toward the café. Passersby ignore them. Click.

One girl has dropped a newspaper. Click.

A man walks by, ignoring the dropped paper. Click.

Two girls sitting at café table. Waiting. No one serves them. Click.

Two girls sitting at café table. The waiter, bored, taking their order. Click.

Carolyn noticed that the waiter didn't look at her or Jay-Cee and took forever to bring them their sodas. They drank them quickly, and — when they finally got the waiter's attention — paid the bill.

It was time to change outfits and go back to the café. Carolyn couldn't wait to put on Jay-Cee's animal-print miniskirt and those spike heels. Jay-Cee was going to do her makeup.

Half an hour later, Carolyn looked at herself in

the mirror. She'd never had on so much makeup. Not even when she and Mandy did makeovers. "I look about twenty!" she exclaimed.

Carolyn and her reflection. Click.

Jay-Cee had put back on what she'd worn to school that day — black capri pants, a short orange sweater, and high-heeled ankle boots.

"CK, you're so tall in those shoes," commented Maya.

CK, thought Carolyn. She never called me that before. I like it.

CK wobbled across the room on high heels.

"Girl," Jay-Cee said, "if you can stay on a horse, you can stay on those shoes. You've got to swing your hips. Watch me." Jay-Cee sashayed across the room. Carolyn found her balance and followed. "That's more like it," Jay-Cee told her. "Now listen to this. If you expect people to pay attention to you, they will. It's not just about how we're dressed. It's about *attitude*. You got it?"

Carolyn stood even taller and put her hands on her hips. "Yeah," she said. "I got it. What's it to you?"

"We better go," said Maya, laughing. "It's getting late."

As Carolyn sashayed down the hall to the elevator, she thought again, I hope I don't run into anyone I know.

They were walking across the lobby when Joy whispered in Carolyn's ear, "I think your father's here."

Carolyn looked toward the front door. It *was* her

father. He was checking the time on his watch as he came into the building.

"Keep going," Joy whispered. "Maybe he won't notice you."

She kept going. But as she was about to pass her father he looked up distractedly and saw the four girls.

At that instant, Carolyn, in mid-sashay, stumbled in the high heels. Recovering her balance on Joy's arm, she and her father came face-to-face. Eye to eye. In heels, she was almost as tall as he was.

"Carolyn?" he gasped. "Wha — what are you doing dressed like that?"

"It's for the photography workshop," she blurted out.

Joy jumped in with an explanation of her project and described what had happened during the first part of the shoot.

"It's really quite scientific, Mr. Kuhlberg," added Maya. "An experiment."

"I see," he said thoughtfully. "I agree with your premise, Joy. I think people do judge others too much by appearance." He hesitated, glancing again at Carolyn and Jay-Cee. "I guess it's all right as long as you girls go right home and change to your regular clothes as soon as you're done."

Maya and Joy exchanged a glance. They were thinking the same thing. These *were* Jay-Cee's regular clothes. She always dressed like that. Maya swallowed hard to keep from laughing.

"We'd better go," said Joy. "Before we lose the light."

"Or the waiter," added Maya. "To be scientific, we need to have the same one."

"Of course," Mr. Kuhlberg agreed.

Two girls walking down the street. A guy walking by smiles at them. Click.

A tourist with a map of New York City asks the girls a question. Click.

One girl drops a newspaper. Click.

A man passing, picks the newspaper up for her. Click.

The girls at a café table. The waiter, smiling, is taking their order. Click.

As the smiling waiter put a soda down in front of Carolyn, she thought, Joy was right. We are being treated differently. And I like it.

He leaned toward the table. "Anything else, girls?" he asked. "We've got a fresh blackout chocolate cake."

Jay-Cee smiled at him. "That's all, thank you."

Carolyn made eye contact. "Just the check, please." *Click.*

The four girls met around the corner from the café. Joy showed them the photos she'd taken on the camera's little screen. Carolyn stared at her more dressed-up, made-up self. It was kind of fun to look glamorous and older. Do I want to look that way more often? she wondered.

"Jay-Cee and I have to go," announced Maya.

She didn't tell them she was having a sleepover with Shana and Delores that night. Or that the reason they weren't invited was because Shana didn't like them.

"I need to give you back your shoes, Jay-Cee," Carolyn remembered. "And the skirt."

"The shoes aren't mine," Jay-Cee said. "I borrowed them from Remember Me. You can return them the next time you're uptown. You can keep the skirt for a couple of weeks. Wear it around. If anyone says they like it, tell them it's a Jay-Cee original."

"Thanks," said Carolyn. When I'm staying at Maya's house, maybe I'll wear it to school, she thought. It isn't really so short. Maya has a skirt that length.

"You should have business cards," Joy was telling Jay-Cee. "If you want, I can make you some on my computer."

"Yeah?" asked Jay-Cee, pleased. "You'd do that?"

Joy nodded. "You design it. I'll print it."

Jay-Cee hugged her. "Thanks."

Jay-Cee and Maya went into the subway and Joy took the crosstown bus.

Carolyn stood alone on the street. Looking to her right, she caught her own reflection in a store window. She liked being taller.

An older guy was passing between her and her reflection. He stopped and looked from one to the other, ending on the real Carolyn. Their eyes met. "Nice," he murmured before moving on.

Carolyn felt herself flush.

As he continued down the street, he looked over his shoulder and winked at her.

She looked away. "Don't make eye contact with anyone," her father had cautioned. She followed that rule all the way home.

When Maya came into the workshop on Saturday, the class was already sitting around the table. "Sorry I'm late," Maya said as she joined them. "The subway took forever."

"Forever?" Beth said with a smirk. "It's a miracle you made it at all then."

A few people laughed, including Maya. Carolyn made room for Maya between herself and Joy. "We're looking at Beth's photo journal," she whispered. "She's showing us, as an example of how to do ours."

Maya saw now that Beth was holding up an opened photo album. "There are some pages that are real personal, so I took those out." She turned the page. "Maybe I'll show them to you later, when we're working with fantasy and dreams."

How do you photograph dreams? wondered Carolyn.

Joy wasn't paying attention to what Beth was saying. All her focus was on the photographs Beth had taken of New York City after the terrorist attacks on the World Trade Center.

A crushed fire truck.

People walking uptown, covered in gray ash.

Beth's baby, Mike, smiling at the camera.

Close-up of a woman, tears streaking her dirt-covered face.

Baby Mike on hands and knees, smiling.

Outside a firehouse. A memorial of candles, flowers, and photos of the missing.

An American flag stuck in a pile of rubble.

"Why do you think I have the photos of my son with images of tragedy?" Beth asked the class.

"Because it was all going on at the same time?" answered Janice. "He was a happy baby and this horrible thing had just happened."

"That's right," agreed Beth. "When he's older, he can look at this book and see himself. It will help me describe it to him."

Joy remembered that Jake was also only a couple of months old when the Twin Towers fell. When he grows up, will I tell him I had a perfect view of the World Trade Center from my bedroom window? she wondered. How I was brushing my hair and looking at those silver towers against the blue sky when the first plane hit? That I saw the explosion when the second plane hit? And the towers collapsing? That I closed my blinds that day and didn't look out the window again for seven months?

"Joy, are you all right?" Maya whispered.

Joy smiled at her gratefully and nodded.

Beth closed the photo album. "I'll pass it around during the break. But now, let's hear how your projects are coming along." She nodded in Carolyn's

85

direction. "We haven't heard anything about your project, why don't you begin."

"I don't think it's very good," admitted Carolyn. "But I thought it was when I started."

"Do you have photos to show?" asked Beth, interrupting her.

Carolyn showed the twelve photos of Ivy she'd chosen to put in her journal. She was surprised at how much time the class took looking at them. There were lots of comments and questions.

Beth held up the photo of Ivy throwing her head back as she hit a pot with her fist. "Great shot," she said. "What else do you want to know about her, Carolyn?"

"I wonder where she lives," Carolyn heard herself answer. "What it looks like. And why she has that tattoo on her wrist. What does it mean to her? Does she have a dog herself? Where else does she drum?"

"I wonder what she was like when she was younger?" Charlie added. "I mean, did she always like animals?"

"Did she play in the school band or something, like on a real bass drum?" asked a girl who hardly ever spoke up during the workshop sessions.

"Can you show all that in photos?" Carolyn asked Beth.

"You won't know unless you try," answered Beth.

Maya threw her backpack over her shoulder and ran up the block. "Alex said he'd be at Zeus around three," she called over her shoulder to Carolyn and

Joy, who were rushing to catch up. "I want to be there when he gets there."

"Why do you want to get there first?" asked Joy.

"I want to photograph how Wren treats him," explained Maya. "Serge told me Alex has this massive crush on her."

"That's news," said Carolyn.

Joy flashed Carolyn a grin. "When did you talk to Serge?" she asked Maya. They were crossing Avenue A.

"Last night," answered Maya. "He called me. He's not going to be at Zeus today. He has to help his uncle with something."

Safely on the other side of the avenue, Maya started running again. She wouldn't tell Carolyn and Joy that Serge had wanted to keep talking to her. *To practice my English*, he'd said. That she would have liked to have talked to him some more, but she had to go because Shana, Delores, and Jay-Cee were there, listening in on her side of the conversation. Shana had teased her after the call. "Was that your boyfriend?" she'd asked. "Your *white* boyfriend?" Shana tried to make it seem like friendly teasing. But Maya knew it wasn't.

After her friends left in the morning, Maya had gone down to her grandmother's apartment. Maybe Gran can help me understand Shana, she'd thought. She knows Shana.

Josie was in her front room waiting for a client. "An Aquarius, like you," she'd said.

Maya explained her problem with Shana. "She's still my best friend, Gran," she concluded, "but she's acting so rude to my other friends." Maya had expected her grandmother to look something up on her astrological chart or give her some practical advice about how to handle Shana. But all Josie had time to say was, "Make new friends but keep the old. One is silver and the other gold."

Tell that to Shana, thought Maya as she pushed the door open into Zeus. She was disappointed to see that Alex was already there, at the counter with Wren. She took out her camera.

Alex and Wren, arm in arm, tongues sticking out. Click.

"How does it feel now, Alex?" Maya asked.

"Ith fine," he answered. "I can eath now."

Joy rolled her eyes at Carolyn. Alex was lisping so bad it was hard to understand him.

Wren laughed. "Ith thath tho."

Alex frowned.

"Don't worry, Al," she said. "It won't sound like that forever. Just six months."

Alex's eyes bulged with alarm. "Thith month?"

"She's just kidding," Joy put in. "That pamphlet said you might lisp for a couple of weeks."

"Not months," added Carolyn.

"The chick clique is so helpful," Wren observed. She turned to Alex. "Ivan's waiting for you."

Alex and Maya went to the back for the appointment.

Joy felt Wren staring at her. Determined not to be intimidated by her, she stared back and asked, "What?"

"Maybe Mommy and Daddy won't let you get pierced," she answered, "but you could do something interesting with your hair."

"Like what?" challenged Joy.

Wren finally broke their locked gaze to study Joy's face and hair.

"Well, I think with your coloring, you'd look good with a lavender streak. And it's a good length for spiking." She reached over the counter and pulled up a handful of Joy's hair. "Yeah. That'd work. I've got what you need."

Wren turned to the shelf behind her for a can of spray hair color and a tube of gel.

"You going to buy it?" Carolyn asked Joy.

"I guess," Joy said back. "Why not?"

While Joy made her purchases, Wren asked Carolyn what she was doing for her photography project. Carolyn told her about Ivy, her dogs, and the Big Bang Band.

"I know the Big Bang Band," she said. "That Ivy is wild." She twirled her thumb ring around. "Where do you guys live, anyway?"

"I live on West Eighty-second Street," Carolyn answered.

"What about you, Joyful?" Wren asked. "You look like a downtown girl to me."

As Joy was thinking, I used to live downtown

half the time, Carolyn answered Wren's question. "She lives just across town from me."

"On East Eighty-second Street?" asked Wren.

"East Seventy-eighth between Third and Lex," answered Carolyn, proud that she said it like a real New Yorker.

Wren looked over at Joy. "Are you in that big white brick building on the corner?"

Joy was surprised that Wren knew her block so well. "No. The redbrick building in the middle," she answered.

"It's fancy up there," said Wren. "You must be rich."

Joy shot her a hard look.

"That's not an insult," Wren said. "Nothing wrong with having a little money." For the first time since they'd met Wren, she smiled. "You really should do your hair the way I said."

Alex and Maya came back up front. Wren turned her smile to Alex. He smiled back.

Joy followed Carolyn and Maya out of the store.

Do Maya and Carolyn have plans? she wondered. Do they include me? Or are they just going to take the West Side train uptown together and I'll get on the East Side train? Should I go uptown on their train and take the bus across town? Maybe they don't want me around at all? She hated this familiar nervous feeling.

Walking slowly down the street, they talked about Wren and Alex and the pictures Maya had taken.

"Do you think Ivy would let me take picures of her apartment?" Carolyn asked.

"I think she will," Maya answered. "She seemed friendly enough. She even wants to see the pictures you took."

"Call and ask," suggested Joy. "Call her now."

"You have your dad's cell phone," Maya reminded her.

"I can't use his phone," Carolyn explained. "Ivy's number will be in his phone log. He's always checking it now. Because of Ivan calling."

Joy pulled her cell phone out of a pocket. "Use mine," she offered. "We can stop at that place across the street, and you can organize the whole thing."

Carolyn took the phone and checked her watch. "I told my dad I'd be home by five, so it'll have to be quick."

"I have to go home soon, too," added Maya.

They crossed the street to the café.

After they all ordered hot chocolate, Carolyn took out Ivy's card.

"She lives in Washington Heights," noticed Maya. "That's up near me."

"If she says I can go to her apartment, I'll do it when I'm staying at your house," said Carolyn.

"We can always do it after school," agreed Maya.

Carolyn smiled. "Perfect." As she dialed Ivy's number, she thought, Dad will never have to know.

Joy swirled the whipped cream around in her hot

chocolate and thought, When Carolyn's staying at Maya's, they'll be together all the time. What about me?

"I hope she's home," Carolyn said as the phone rang for the fourth time.

Someone picked up on the next ring. "Hello. Ivy here," Ivy announced.

Carolyn told her that she had a set of photos for her.

"What's your apartment number?" asked Ivy. "I can come by Monday before I pick up the dogs."

Not a good idea, thought Carolyn. My dad will be there. "I leave for school pretty early," she told Ivy.

"Tell her you'll leave them with your doorman," whispered Joy.

"I can leave them with our doorman," Carolyn told Ivy. Then she asked if she could take pictures of Ivy at home.

"My apartment's pretty small and nothing special," she answered, "unless you think having the bathtub in the kitchen is cool."

"That *is* cool," agreed Carolyn.

They arranged a photo shoot for four o'clock the next Wednesday.

"Her bathtub's in the kitchen!" Carolyn exclaimed when she'd hung up.

Maya laughed. "Some of the old New York apartments have that. They're usually pretty small. The apartments, not the tubs."

"I can't wait to see it," Carolyn said as she flipped

through her appointment book to write down her meeting with Ivy.

Joy saw STAYING AT MAYA'S neatly printed at the top of one page after another.

Carolyn's father wasn't home when she got there. Why did he tell me to be in by five if he wasn't going to be here? she wondered. She was sitting on her bed putting together a set of photos for Ivy when she heard the door open. Quickly putting the photos back in her bedside table drawer, she called out, "Hi, Dad."

"Hello," he answered. "I didn't think you'd be home yet."

She glanced at her clock radio. It was five-thirty. He'd told her to be home by five. That's weird, she thought. Doesn't he remember when he told me to be home? He's always so strict about time and always checking his watch.

As she walked into the living room/kitchen, she saw him going into his room with two big shopping bags. She followed him in.

"What'd you get?" she asked.

"Nothing much," he answered. "Just some clothes for my business trip to Thailand." He looked embarrassed. "It's warm there. Well, I haven't bought any clothes since — in a long time."

He means he hasn't bought any clothes since Mom died, she thought. She suddenly felt sorry for her dad. She'd lost a wonderful mother, but he'd lost a wonderful wife. A wife who, Carolyn remembered, helped him shop for clothes. She wondered what her father had picked out for himself.

"You going to show me what you bought?" she asked.

"All right," he agreed. "If you want to see them."

He showed her a lightweight navy suit, three colorful ties, three shirts — two light blue and one pale yellow — a pair of casual pants, two white polo shirts, and a green cotton sweater. She thought of her father as always wearing shades of brown and beige.

"There was an excellent sale," he explained.

The clothes were neatly piled on his bed now. It must have been sad to shop all by himself, she thought. Poor old Dad. But he had picked out good-looking things. "You did a great job, Dad."

"Yes," he said quietly. "I guess I did." He smiled at her. "You know, I'll miss you, but I'm really looking forward to this trip. I haven't traveled for work since we moved here. I know you'll be in good hands with the Johnsons."

"I will," she agreed. She was happy that her father was going on a trip, too. Next week, she'd be staying at Maya's.

Washington Heights

Joy wandered around the apartment. She started in the living room, with its big white couches and leather armchairs. From there she walked through the dining room, past the long table. She couldn't remember the last time she and her mother had eaten in the dining room. They always ate at the kitchen table — mostly take-out. *I get home from work too late to think about cooking,* her mother would say. Or, *I have more important things to do than cook.*

The *important* thing her mother was doing tonight was producing a television commercial for a designer perfume called Real. *Real* expensive, thought Joy. I'm glad Maya doesn't know what my mother does for a living. Maya always says the media tries to get people to spend money for things they don't need. Like overpriced perfume.

Joy got a juice from the refrigerator and walked down the hall — past her mother's bedroom to her own. It was Tuesday and she hadn't heard from Carolyn and Maya all week. Carolyn was staying at Maya's while her father was on his business trip. Joy imagined how much fun they must be having —

hanging out with Maya's friends, doing homework to-gether, and talking into the night. Tomorrow, after school, Carolyn and Maya were going to take pictures in Ivy's apartment. Maya would go with her for sure. All week, Joy had hoped that Carolyn would call and invite her to go, too. But she hadn't. They never in-vited her to do stuff during the week.

Why? she wondered. Sometimes I think they like me. Then sometimes I think they don't. I hate feel-ing like this.

Joy picked up the pile of photos she had printed out for Jay-Cee and flipped through them. Would they help Jay-Cee get modeling jobs? Were they good enough? I should look at them on the computer with her, Joy decided. Then she can tell me if she wants them edited. I could darken them, lighten them, crop them in different ways.

She sat on her couch and stared out at the city-lit sky. It was so quiet in the apartment she could hear herself breathing. Sometimes the apartment was too quiet. She put on the CD she'd bought of the Big Bang Band. She listened to the music and thought, I should have a party. A sleepover party. I'll invite Car-olyn and Maya and Jay-Cee. We can work on Jay-Cee's portfolio pictures and look at the photos for my project.

She reached for the phone. The first thing she had to do was call her mother for permission. She turned down the music and dialed her mother's cell phone number.

Her mother said she could have the party. "As long as there are just the four of you. I have a date on Friday, so I'll be out late."

Next, she called Maya.

Carolyn answered. "Johnson residence."

"Hi," said Joy, suddenly shy. What if no one wanted to come to her sleepover? What if they had other plans? "It's me. Joy. There's something I have to ask you and Maya."

Maya got on the other phone so they could have a three-way conversation. She and Carolyn said that a sleepover would be fun and that, yes, they'd love to come. "We can all go to the workshop together from your place," Carolyn suggested.

"Exactly," agreed Joy.

Maya was thinking, When Shana hears that Jay-Cee was invited to a party and she wasn't, she'll be upset. "Are you going to invite Delores and Shana, too?" she asked Joy.

Joy's first thought was, Why not? Then she remembered why not and told Maya her mother had said there could only be four of them.

"My mother would be the same way if she wasn't going to be there," admitted Maya. Meanwhile, she thought, I better tell Jay-Cee to keep the party a secret.

A strong feeling of danger rolled through Maya. Something bad is going to happen, she thought. Something to do with Joy's party. The dark thought went from her as quickly as it had come, but it left a tingling feeling along her forearms.

"Are you playing Ivy's CD?" Carolyn asked Joy.

"Yeah," said Joy. "I love it."

"Let's play it at your party," suggested Maya. "It'll be fun to dance to."

Next, Joy called Jay-Cee, who said she'd come to the party, too. "I made your skirt," she said. "I'll bring it."

When Joy hung up, she looked around her room. Twin beds and a couch that opened into a double bed. Her room was perfect for a four-girl sleepover. The apartment didn't seem so empty now. She started a list of what she'd need for her party. Pizza was at the top.

The first thing Carolyn noticed about Ivy's apartment was that it was only one room — a really small room. The second thing she noticed was that the whole apartment was painted in shades of blue — walls, ceiling, cabinets — all blue.

"I've lived here ten years," said Ivy. "Since I was twenty-five."

"Look," Maya whispered. She pointed to a yellow bird flying around the room. It landed on the curtain rod.

"That's Cheapy," said Ivy. "Spelled c-h-e-a-p. He was so cheap, he was free. I found him in the church cemetery last year. Must have escaped from someone's apartment. He would have died. I sort of had to save him." She looked up and called, "Cheapy." He flew off the rod.

Cheapy on Ivy's head. Click.

"Should I give you a tour?" Ivy asked.

"Okay," Carolyn agreed, suddenly wondering if there were more rooms after all. But there weren't.

Ivy reached up and grabbed Cheapy. "Back in the cage with you."

Cheapy in his cage. Click.

Ivy gestured to her right. "The kitchen."

A half-sized stove and blue refrigerator. Click.

Ivy lifted the blue wood top off what Carolyn thought was a low, long table against the wall. It was the bathtub. *Click.*

Ivy turned to face the rest of the room, which she called her bedroom/living room/studio.

A single bed, small blue bureau, and electronic drum. Click.

Ivy squeezed past Maya to stand in front of the only window in the apartment. "The best thing about this apartment is the window," she said as she opened it. "Look at the view."

Carolyn leaned out the window and looked around. "Wow!" she whispered. She was facing the back of a church and an old graveyard. The grass between the tombstones was covered with a carpet of fallen autumn leaves. It was hard to believe they were still in New York City. Bird sounds came from a tree whose branches hung over the fire escape. Cheapy answered their song with his own.

Carolyn felt Ivy looking over her shoulder. "I love

living behind a cemetery," she said. "I'm part Chero-
kee Indian. I was raised to respect the dead. Their
spirits comfort and inspire me."

Carolyn wanted to tell Ivy that her mother's spirit
sometimes comforted and inspired her. Instead she
said, "Can I take your picture out on the fire escape?"

As Ivy climbed out the window, Carolyn had a
close-up view of her wrist tattoo. It's not barbed wire,
she realized. It's an ivy plant with small leaves.

*Close-up of Ivy on fire escape. Gravestones in
background. Click.*

Carolyn hoped that her photo would show Ivy's
feeling for the spirits of the dead.

After school on Friday, Joy shopped for her
party. Walking home, she noticed that the apartment
building on the corner wasn't white brick. Wren had
been wrong about that. Thinking about Wren reminded Joy of the hair color and gel Wren had sold
her. Maybe she'd use it for the party. If it looked stupid, she could always wash it out.

The doorman held the front door open for her. "I
have some friends coming over in a little while," she
told him. "You can send them right up."

"Certainly, Miss Benoit," he said with a nod.

While Joy unlocked the door to the apartment,
Paget Sandler opened her door across the hall. "Getting ready for your party?" she asked.

"Yes," said Joy as she wondered, How does Ms.
Sandler know I'm having a party? She's a mystery

book writer, so she's smart about clues. But what clues? Two grocery bags? Joy picked them up. Did Ms. Sandler notice they were heavy and guess that there were two big bottles of soda? Joy turned. Her neighbor was still in the doorway, watching her.

"You're wondering how I know you're having a party," she said.

"Yes," answered Joy. She was now convinced that her busybody neighbor was as good a detective as her main character — Prairie Peters.

Ms. Sandler laughed. "Your mother told me. She said you were having three friends for a sleepover and that I should let you know I was home. In case you need something. She's left you a note to that effect."

Joy found her mother's note and money for the pizza on the kitchen table. She put the food away, turned on some music, and changed into jeans and a black long-sleeved top. It was time to spike her hair with gel and spray on lavender hair color. She took off her little diamond-and-emerald ring. It was her favorite piece of jewelry, and she didn't want to get color and goop all over it.

She sprayed. She gelled. She spiked.

Studying the results in the bathroom mirror, she decided too much goo. Too much color.

She washed it all out and started over again. The second time around she liked it enough to leave it.

She was emptying chips into a bowl when the intercom buzzed.

She ran to the hall and pressed LISTEN.

"Three guests are on the way up, Miss Benoit," the doorman announced.

Joy opened the door and waited for them. She felt jittery. It was the first party she'd had since fourth grade. And the first one ever when her parents weren't there. What if it turned out to be a bad idea? What if it turned out to be a rotten party?

When Carolyn saw Joy she exclaimed, "I love your hair like that."

"Me, too," added Maya as she handed Joy a bouquet of daisies. "These are from me and Carolyn."

Jay-Cee gave her a Remember Me shopping bag. "It's the skirt I designed for you. It'll look great with that hair and top."

"Thanks," said Joy. "Come on in." She didn't feel nervous anymore. This was going to be a great party.

She put the flowers in a vase and tried on the skirt. Jay-Cee made her walk up and down the living room and turn around slowly. "I was right," she announced with satisfaction. "It's perfect on you."

Carolyn was glad she was wearing a skirt Jay-Cee designed, too.

Back in her bedroom, Joy checked out her reflection again. Jay-Cee was right. The tulip-cut denim skirt looked great on her.

Joy grinned at Jay-Cee. "Thank you. I love it." She paused. "I hope you like your pictures."

Joy sat in front of the computer. Jay-Cee was in

her rolling desk chair. Carolyn and Maya stood behind them. Joy clicked on the file: *Jay-Cee's Model Pics.*

Jay-Cee liked the pictures and only wanted changes on two.

Next, Joy showed them the photos she and Maya took at the café.

Carolyn loved looking at herself in the After pictures. "Clothes and makeup make such a difference," she said thoughtfully.

"Yeah, but so does attitude," put in Maya. "If you had been all smiles and friendly acting with the waiter that first time, I bet he would have treated you at least a little bit better."

"Maybe," agreed Carolyn.

"But sometimes you *want* to be alone, even when you're in a crowd," added Jay-Cee. "When I feel like that, I throw on any old thing. Something really dull. I walk around pretending I'm your normal everyday kind of girl instead of the luscious, talented babe I really am." She turned herself around in the chair.

Joy remembered the guy ogling her breasts on the subway. Jay-Cee was right. Sometimes you want to hide your body.

"Is anyone hungry?" she asked. "Want to order pizza?"

"Yes!" they answered in unison.

They chose toppings and Joy phoned in the order. Meanwhile Jay-Cee put on a CD she'd brought, and they danced to hip-hop.

"Let's put color in Carolyn's hair," Jay-Cee suggested. "The lavender will look great with her red."

Carolyn thought, Dad will never see it, so why not? "All right," she agreed.

Jay-Cee sprayed and spiked until she was satisfied. I like it, thought Carolyn. It's fun hair, like Ivy's when she performed at the street fair.

The intercom buzzed.

"A delivery from the pizzeria, Miss Benoit," the doorman announced over the speaker.

"Send him up," answered Joy.

"There are more guests here," he added. "They are coming up, too."

More guests? thought Joy. It must be Shana and Delores. Maya must have told them about the party, and they decided to crash it. I can't turn them away. That would be so lame. "Shana and Delores are here," she told Maya. "I'm glad we ordered two pies."

"I didn't tell them about your party," said Maya, surprised. "How did they know you were having one?" They both looked at Jay-Cee, who was dancing with Carolyn in the living room.

Joy got out the money for the pizza plus a tip for the delivery guy. She'd be friendly and ignore the fact that Shana and Delores weren't invited. After all, they were Maya's best friends. She was smiling when she opened the door and faced the pizza delivery guy. Behind him stood Serge, Alex, and Wren.

She was speechless.

But Wren wasn't. She was already in the apartment saying, "Wow. This is one fancy place."

"How'd you know where we were?" Maya asked Serge. She wanted Joy to know that she hadn't told *him* about the party, either.

"Wren wanted to go to this cool secondhand clothing store in Harlem," answered Alex. He rubbed the front of the aqua '50s sports shirt he was wearing. "You like it? Wren picked it out."

The shirt had a thin peach-colored stripe. Maya recognized it. It was from her mother's store. She told everyone about the coincidence.

"Remember Me is your store?" exclaimed Wren. "That's cool." She looked from Joy to Carolyn. "You guys get free clothes?"

"We get a discount," announced Carolyn proudly.

Wren put an arm around Maya's shoulder. "I'm your friend, too," she said. "Right?"

Maya and Joy exchanged a glance that said, No, you're not.

The pizza guy cleared his throat. "Your pizza. Somebody's pizza. Anybody's pizza," he said to whoever would listen.

Serge took the pizza. Joy paid for it. Pizza Guy left.

"I didn't know it was your mother's store," Serge told Maya. "We were in your neighborhood. I called your house telephone number because maybe you wanted to see us."

Wren looked up from going through the CDs. "Anyway, whoever answered the phone at your place told Serge you were here, and I remembered where 'here' was. So here we are." She looked straight into Joy's eyes. "I know we're wicked party crashers. But hey, sometimes those are the people that make the party a *party*." She looked around at the others. "Let's dance!"

Serge and Joy went into the kitchen with the pizza.

"I am sorry that we came without telling you," Serge said, smiling. He put the pizza on the kitchen table. "Is it a very bad surprise?"

"It's okay," she said. She didn't want to say that she was supposed to have only three people at her party. It sounded so childish. She'd just be sure the party crashers left before her mother came home.

The volume on the stereo went up. But above the music, Joy could hear the happy voices in her living room. She opened a package of paper plates. Maybe Wren was right, she thought. Maybe the people who crash a party make it better.

Maya came into the kitchen looking for her camera. "I'm going to take more pictures of Alex," she announced. "And some of Wren's piercings, too. My project may be about both of them." She found her camera on the counter and left.

"Alex thinks Wren is the most special girl in the world," commented Serge.

"Is she?" asked Joy.

He opened the pizza box without answering her. The smells of pepperoni, mushroom, tomato, and cheese filled the air; music and voices surrounded Joy. This is turning into such a great party, she thought. Friends. Food. Music. Boys!

"Wren is not special all the time," Serge finally said, answering her question. "But she is very fun. And funny."

Funny ha-ha or funny weird? wondered Joy. As if to answer the question, laughter rolled in from the living room.

Joy handed the plates and some napkins to Serge. "You bring out the pizza, and I'll get the soda."

After they ate, Carolyn and Serge moved the coffee table to make more room for dancing. Wren put on the Big Bang Band CD and pulled Alex up to dance with her.

Maya looked through her camera lens.

Wren and Alex dancing. Click.

Close-up on Wren's belly-button ring. Click.

Close-up on the snake tattoo on Wren's lower back. Click.

Serge and Joy jumping and stomping to the music. Click.

Serge with his arms around Jay-Cee and Carolyn. Click.

"Alex is going to get another piercing in his tongue," Wren suddenly announced to everyone.

"I am?" said Alex.

Carolyn thought he looked startled — like the

deer she'd seen surprised by the vehicle headlights on the ranch roads at night.

Wren threw an arm around his shoulder. "Ah, Alex, you'd do it for me, wouldn't you?"

"I guess," agreed Alex. "You really think it would be cool?"

She kissed him on the lips — in front of everyone. Carolyn wondered if their barbells could get caught. Wren whispered something in his ear. He nodded and started to break-dance. All the curves of Alex's body turned into angles. Jutting, folding, moving angles. He dropped to the floor and spun around on his shoulders.

Alex jumping up from a shoulder stand. Click.

"Alex is so good with the breaking dance," Serge told Maya. When Alex finished, they hooted and clapped. He pulled Carolyn up from the couch.

Carolyn and Alex dancing. Click.

Joy and Serge dancing. Click.

Why is Alex dancing with me instead of Wren? wondered Carolyn. She looked around. Where was Wren? She caught Joy's eye and mouthed, *Where's Wren?*

Joy was thinking about Wren, too. She'd seen her leave the room when Alex started break-dancing. She figured Wren had gone to the bathroom. But that was a while ago, and she wasn't back. Was she all right? What if she was sick, throwing up in the bathroom? Joy knew that happened at parties. But there wasn't drinking at this party. While the others kept dancing, she went to look for her.

Wren wasn't in the bathroom.

Joy looked for her in her mother's room and bathroom. Not there, either.

She stopped at the doorway to her own room. Wren was standing at her bureau.

"What are you doing?" Joy asked.

Wren turned to her. "Nothing. Just checking out your room. I used your bathroom. This is a nice room." She took a few steps toward Joy. "The guys and me — we gotta go. Another party."

Joy glanced at the top of her bureau. Her jewelry box, a brush, and some change were there. And a novel she'd been reading.

She felt her left pinkie finger. No ring.

The thought *I left the ring Uncle Brett gave me on the bureau* popped into her head. *I remember taking it off before I did my hair. I didn't put it back on. Where is it?*

Wren's right hand was clutched closed. Joy's heart pounded.

She has my ring. She's stealing my ring. What am I going to do?

East 78TH Street

Joy kept her eye on Wren's closed hand.

"So thanks for letting us crash your party," Wren said as she started to walk past Joy.

Joy grabbed her arm. "Wait. You have my ring. Give it back."

"What ring?" Wren laughed. "What are you talking about?"

Joy looked at Wren's still-clutched right hand. "Open your hand, then. Prove you don't have it."

Wren locked eyes with her. Joy didn't look away. Thoughts screamed in her head.

I'm such a jerk. I never should have let her and those guys crash my party. She has my ring. The ring Uncle Brett gave me. How do I get it back?

"Do you want to fight?" asked Wren. "Is that what you want?" A stiff little smile twisted her mouth.

Fight? I've never been in a fight. I don't know how to fight. She could hurt me.

Joy dropped Wren's arm and said sharply, "I know you have my ring. If you don't give it back —"

Wren pushed past her and walked into the hall.

"You rich girls are all so paranoid. Like everybody wants your stuff."

Joy followed her. "Give me back my ring and I won't call the police," she said firmly. "No one will know but you and me."

Wren turned to her. "You're crazy. You're imagining things."

Maybe she's right. Maybe I put my ring in my jewelry box. Or left it in the bathroom. No. I put it on the bureau. I remember doing it.

They'd reached the living room now.

Should I tell everyone that she stole my ring? Should I call the police?

"Alex, Serge," Wren shouted above the music. "We gotta go. Now." Both boys came over to her. Wren put her arm around Alex.

I have to do something. I have to do it now.

She stepped up to Wren. "You stole my ring!" Joy shouted in her face.

Everyone stopped in mid-action. Like that game of statues, thought Carolyn.

Maya broke her pose and asked, "What's going on?"

Carolyn turned down the music.

"My ring was on the bureau," explained Joy. "Wren took it. And she won't give it back." Joy could hear her own voice — strong and serious. She didn't know how, but she was going to get her ring back. Wren wasn't going to get away with it.

"The one your uncle gave you?" asked Carolyn.

Joy nodded. "She has it in her hand."

Wren held up both her hands and slowly opened them — empty. "Girl, you are par-a-noid. It's embar-rassing." She opened the front door and stepped into the hall outside the apartment. Alex followed her.

"Thanks for the party," Wren said sweetly. "It was *swell*."

"What is 'bureau'?" Serge asked anxiously. No one answered him.

Joy stood in the doorway. Suddenly, she remembered Wren putting her arm around Alex. In one big step, Joy was at his side, reaching into the back pocket of his jeans. She took out her ring, put it on her finger, and held up her hand. "There," she said.

"Huh?" Alex asked, confused.

"Thanks, Alex," Wren said angrily. "Thanks a lot."

The door across the hall opened and Ms. Sandler came out.

Joy saw her take in everything at a glance. Wren and Alex hurrying down the hall. Carolyn's red-and-lavender hair and miniskirt. Her own dyed, spiked hair. Serge with his purple-streaked bleached hair, four piercings, and T-shirt that read ZEUS.

Joy turned to Serge. It was his fault. "You, too. Out."

"I am not robbing," Serge said to anyone who would listen.

"You brought them here," Maya hissed in his ear. "Go."

He nodded and said, "Good evening, ma'am," to Ms. Sandler. And left.

"Your mother said that there would only be three girls," Paget Sandler said. She looked from Carolyn to Maya to Jay-Cee. "That would be you three, I presume."

Joy, remembering her manners, introduced the three girls and told them that Paget Sandler was a famous mystery writer.

"My mother loved your books!" exclaimed Carolyn. "She was always talking about that detective. . . ."

"Prairie Peters," Joy finished.

The author lightly touched Carolyn's arm. "Thank you for telling me. Maybe you'll be a fan someday, too."

She knows Carolyn's mother is dead, thought Maya. She figured it out because Carolyn said her mother *loved* her books. That was the clue.

"I can lend you my copies, Carolyn," offered Joy. "I have them all." She smiled at her famous neighbor. "They're all autographed."

Ms. Sandler didn't smile back. "Your mother didn't mention that you were having *gents* at your party, Joy."

"I wasn't," explained Joy. "They tried to crash it. We told them to leave."

"But you knew that boy," said Paget. "The one with manners and all the piercings. And why were those others rushing off?"

"They were in a hurry," said Carolyn, trying to help.

"I know them from a project I'm doing for our photo workshop," added Maya. "I photographed them. It's sort of my fault they came."

"But you must have told the doorman to let them in," Paget told Joy, following one clue to the next. "He'd never let them come up without buzzing you first."

"It was all a big mistake," admitted Joy. "I'm sorry we bothered you."

Mrs. Sandler looked past Joy into the apartment. "Do you have anyone else hiding in there?" she asked, smiling again.

"No," answered Joy.

"Well, dear, you tell your mother about all these goings-on yourself," she said. "I'm not your chaperon, after all. Just the friendly neighbor available if you need something."

"Thank you, Mrs. Sandler," Joy said.

"Please, call me Paget. And also, call me if any-one else tries to crash your party."

Paget was going back into her apartment when she turned and added, "By the way, I like your hair like that, Joy. I'll give Prairie a new hairdo in this book. You've inspired me."

The instant the four girls were safely back in Joy's apartment, they started talking at once.

"Do you think Wren came here to steal?" asked Carolyn.

"I'm so mad at Serge for bringing those guys," said Maya angrily.

"I don't think Mrs. Sandler will tell my mother," Joy said with relief.

"That guy Alex was cute," Jay-Cee was saying. "But *what* is he doing with that Wren girl? Bad choice."

Joy held up her hand to quiet the others.

"What?" asked Maya.

"Maybe Wren stole something else," she said.

They all ran to Joy's room. She looked through the jewelry box on her bureau. The pearl earrings her mother gave her were still there. So was the diamond-drop necklace from her father. The silver earrings and bracelet her aunt Leslie sent from Santa Fe were there, too. She had on her watch.

"Nothing's missing," she announced with relief.

"Did Wren go into your mother's room?" asked Carolyn.

Fear shot through Joy again. Her mother had valuable jewelry. Did Wren take something? *Please, no!* She was already halfway to her mother's room.

Maya switched on the overhead light.

Joy opened a drawer. She held her breath and reached into the back. The jewelry box was there. And it was locked. She looked around the room. Perfectly neat. Everything in place.

"I don't think she got anything," Joy announced to her friends.

"Girl, you just took on that Wren fool," Jay-Cee said. "Just told her, *Gimme my ring.* Wow."

"Taking that ring out of Alex's pocket was smooth," added Maya.

"I'd have been so scared," added Carolyn.

"I was," admitted Joy.

She noticed her reflection in her mother's full-length mirror and thought, I have a great new skirt and lavender-spiked hair. The party crashers are gone. The real party can begin.

Her friends were in the mirror, too. She grinned at their reflections and said, "This is a pajama party. What do you want to do next?"

They all looked at one another in the mirror.

"Get into our pajamas," suggested Maya.

Carolyn tried to run her fingers through her colored, stiff hair. "I want to get this stuff out," she said.

"I have some great DVDs," added Joy. "My mom has a friend in the movie business. He's always sending me these cool films."

"Do you have any popcorn?" asked Jay-Cee.

Joy and Carolyn took showers while Maya and Jay-Cee made popcorn. When they were all back in Joy's room, Maya finished off her roll of film.

Jay-Cee braiding Carolyn's hair. Click.

Joy painting Carolyn's toenails while Carolyn paints Jay-Cee's toenails. Click.

Carolyn doing a handstand. Click.

They ate the popcorn and watched a movie. When they were on their second movie, Joy's mother came home.

She stood in the doorway to Joy's room and

looked around at the girls lounging in their pajamas. "So sweet," she said. "A storybook sleepover. I love it."

Maya swallowed a giggle and said, "We've had a great time."

Carolyn buried her face in a pillow so Ms. Benoit wouldn't see her laugh.

"Thank you for the pizza," added Jay-Cee.

Ms. Benoit took off her high heels. "Did Mrs. Sandler check in on you?" she asked.

"Yes," the four girls answered in unison.

"She's really nice," added Carolyn.

"Well, I'll leave you to your fun, then," Ms. Benoit said. "Good night."

The girls held their breath still until they heard Ms. Benoit's bedroom door close. Then they all burst into laughter. Carolyn's laughter rolled her right off the couch and onto the floor with a thud.

Jay-Cee did a perfect imitation of Joy's mother asking, *Did Mrs. Sandler check in on you?*

Through guffaws, Maya gasped. "I have to go. I — have — to go." And she ran to the bathroom.

When they finally settled down for the night, they whispered in the dark.

Jay-Cee's voice trailed off in the middle of a sentence.

Joy and Maya talked about what kind of bagels they liked, and how they'd get fresh, hot ones in the morning.

Carolyn stopped listening. Images of the party flashed through her mind. *I had a great time* was her last thought before drifting off to sleep. She didn't answer when Maya asked, "Are you asleep, Carolyn?"

"Jay-Cee's asleep, too," Joy whispered to Maya. "You want to go to sleep?"

"Okay," agreed Maya. "Thanks for the great party. Good night."

"Good night," answered Joy.

Maya watched the pattern of city lights on the ceiling and thought, It *was* a great party. But not all great. The business with Wren was *bad*. Things could have gotten way more out of hand. What if there had been a fight? What if Wren had a knife? I had a bad feeling about the party that I ignored. I should have told Joy not to let Serge and his pals in. She listened to Carolyn's soft snores. *I failed my friends* was her last thought before she fell asleep.

Joy heard Maya's slow, even breaths. She felt extremely tired and very awake at the same time. Her mind raced. *Why can't I fall asleep? My party turned out to be a big success. I think. And everyone seems to like me a little bit more. They think I was brave to challenge Wren and take back my ring.*

Her heart raced.

What if Wren wants to get back at me? She knows where I live.

Joy turned over on her side and felt around on the floor until she found her old teddy bear.

After school on Monday, Maya and Carolyn dropped off the roll of film from the party. An hour later, they stood in front of the photo shop to look at the pack of pictures.

Carolyn pointed to a photo of Alex break-dancing. "That's a cool picture. The way his mouth is open, you can see the barbell on his tongue. It's great for your project."

"You're right," agreed Maya. "It shows something about him besides having a crush on Wren."

"Do you think Alex knew that Wren was going to steal stuff?" asked Carolyn. "That she was up to no good?"

"I don't think so," admitted Maya. "He was really surprised about the ring being in his jeans."

"Joy was so brave to take it out of his pocket," said Carolyn. "It was like a scene out of a movie."

"*The Party Crashers*," added Maya. "I think I'll skip the sequel." She turned to the next photo.

Carolyn in a miniskirt. Lavender streaks in her hair. Joy and Serge on either side of her, arms around her shoulders. All of them laughing.

Carolyn looked at the picture and thought, I was having fun.

The next photo was of Wren and Alex kissing.

"I didn't know you took a picture of *that*," exclaimed Carolyn, laughing.

"I couldn't resist," admitted Maya.

"I bet Alex would like a copy of that one," said Carolyn.

As they flipped through the rest of the pictures, Carolyn thought, I loved that party. It was fun. I love that Serge and Alex came. It's true we made a mistake about Wren. But you can't tell what a person is like by how they dress and whether they have piercings or tattoos. Ivy's nose is pierced. She has five or six earrings in one ear. And she's got a tattoo on her wrist. But she's great. She writes music. She loves animals and believes that people's spirits live on after they die. Like me.

"Can I have the extra set of pictures?" Carolyn asked. "I'll share them with Joy."

"Okay," agreed Maya.

While they walked the couple of blocks to Maya's, three different groups of kids said hi to her. Each time they met a new group, Maya told Carolyn that they were her friends.

"You have so many friends," commented Carolyn as they climbed the steps of Maya's house.

"I've lived in this house all my life," explained Maya. "Harlem is my hometown." She unlocked the door. "I bet you're friends with loads of people in Dubois."

"There aren't loads of people in Dubois," explained Carolyn. She looked up and down Maya's block. "Downtown Dubois is only one street long. Most people live outside of town in houses that are far apart. There were only twenty kids in my grade."

They went into the kitchen for a snack.

Talking about friends reminded Maya of Shana. She hadn't talked to her in days. I'll invite her for a just-the-two-of-us sleepover on Friday night, she decided. When Carolyn is gone.

Hannah came into the kitchen carrying the Candy Land board game. "Will *somebody* play with me?" she begged. "I'm desperate."

Carolyn and Maya exchanged a smile.

"*Desperate?*" said Maya.

"That sounds serious," added Carolyn.

"It *is*," wailed Hannah.

Carolyn took the game from her and put it on the kitchen table. "I'll play with you."

"Only one game, Hannah," warned Maya. She tapped Carolyn's shoulder. "I'm going upstairs. I have to make a phone call."

Carolyn sat facing Hannah. I bet Maya's calling Shana, she thought. Maya and I are becoming good friends. But Shana is her old best friend like Mandy is my old best friend.

Hannah had opened the game board and set out the playing pieces and cards.

As they began the game, Carolyn continued thinking about Mandy. Maybe I'll write to her tonight. But what will I say? What happened at Joy's is too complicated to explain. Besides, she doesn't know any of my New York friends.

She moved her piece.

I wish I could be with Mandy and talk and talk. We used to have such great sleepovers. We shared so many secrets in the dark.

"Your turn again," prompted Hannah.

Carolyn moved her piece.

Three turns later, Mr. Johnson's voice boomed through the kitchen. "Guess who's home?" He swept Hannah off the chair and into his arms. "Could it be your pa?"

"Dad-dy. Dad-dy!" Hannah shrieked. "I'm *winning*."

He looked over the game board. "And so you are." He winked at Carolyn.

Hannah wiggled to get down. "Carolyn's not *letting* me win, Daddy. She's just not very good."

He sat her back in the chair and looked over her shoulder while she made her next move.

Carolyn watched Mr. Johnson watching his daughter. I miss my dad, she thought. He's thousands and thousands of miles away. Tomorrow he's flying home. What if his plane crashes? What if I became a total orphan?

Joy lay on her couch half-watching a sitcom re-run that she'd already seen twice. She'd finished the novel she had to read for English. It was good, but depressing. She sighed. Her mother wouldn't be home for hours. Sometimes, she thought, it's really lonely here.

She looked down at her red-painted toes and wiggled them. Three days had passed since the party, and her mother still didn't know what *really* happened. I'll probably tell her someday. But not now.

She tried to change channels on the remote with

her feet and turned up the volume instead. She sat up and turned the TV off — with her fingers. What are Maya and Carolyn doing tonight? she wondered. Are they doing something with Jay-Cee, Shana, and Delores right now?

She went to the window and looked out. I should have invited Shana and Delores to my party. I could have asked my mom. It was just two more. If they came to my party, maybe they'd start inviting me to do things.

Her cell phone rang.

She found it in her jacket pocket. Maybe it's Maya and Carolyn inviting me to do something after all, she hoped.

"Hi, it's me," said the voice on the other end. Sue.

Joy sat on her bed. "Hello, Sue."

"I haven't seen you in so long, Joy," she said in her cheeriest voice.

Joy rubbed the ear of her old teddy between her thumb and middle finger. Poor old worn-out teddy, she thought. I love you.

"I miss you," continued Sue. "I'm the only woman in a household of men now. I need you to balance things out a little."

You need me to baby-sit, thought Joy.

"Speaking of men," Sue continued, "how's that boyfriend of yours? Is it a one-on-one thing, or do you hang out with a group?"

"We just all hang out," answered Joy.

"So tell me, what's he like?"

"I'm sort of busy, Sue. I have to go."

"Oh, okay," said Sue. "Me, too. Why I called was, it's your father's birthday a week from Friday. We would like you to come here that night. For dinner."

Joy could hear Jake chattering in baby babble in the background.

"I guess it's okay."

"Ma-ma-ma," Jake was saying in the background. "Ba-ba-ba."

"Did you hear that, Joy?" asked Sue. "Jake's talking."

"What's ba-ba-ba?" asked Joy.

"Bottle," answered Sue enthusiastically. "Isn't it wonderful?"

Wonderful, *really* wonderful, Joy thought. He must be a genius.

"Ba-ba-ba," Jake repeated.

"And, Joy," added Sue. "Bring your camera. I'd love it if you'd take pictures. You're becoming the family photographer."

"Sure," she agreed.

Joy said good-bye and closed the phone. She looked down at her teddy bear. "I wish I could just have dinner with Dad," she said. "Just the two of us."

West 82nd Street

The security guard stopped Maya on her way out of the media center. "Are you Maya Johnson?" he asked. When she nodded, he handed her a manila envelope. "This is for you."

As Maya took the envelope from him she wondered, Why would anyone send me something here?

Joy and Carolyn were wondering the same thing. They all went outside to see what it was. MAYA JOHNSON / PHOTOGRAPHY WORKSHOP was written in big red letters across the front. Maya opened the envelope and pulled out a copy of the *Daily News*.

Joy laughed. "It must be from Serge."

"Open it," urged Carolyn. "Hurry."

Maya turned to the centerfold. A message was written on the newsprint in big orange letters.

DEAR MAYA, JOY, AND CAROLYN,

I AM FULL OF SORROW FOR COMING TO THE HOME OF JOY WITHOUT THE INVITATION. IT WAS A BIG MISTAKE. I LEARN THE IMPORTANT LESSON TO NOT TRUST ALL PEOPLE. PLEASE WILL YOU TRUST ME? I TELL YOU ONLY TRUE THINGS. I AM YOUR FRIEND. ALEX IS SORRY ALSO. HE DOES NOT MAKE THE DATES WITH WREN ANYMORE. SERGE.

Carolyn sighed. "That's so sweet."

Joy arched an eyebrow. "Sweet?"

"He feels bad," explained Carolyn. "He didn't know that Wren was going to take stuff."

"The only reason they came to my house was to steal," said Joy.

"Not Serge," protested Maya. "He didn't know what she was up to. Alex, either."

"Then those guys are really naive," said Joy.

"And so were we," added Maya. She folded the newspaper. "Should we forgive Serge?"

"Yes," said Carolyn.

Joy nodded.

"Should we tell him he's forgiven?" Maya asked.

Joy nodded again. "Let's write him a message now and drop it off at his building."

A chilling wind blew through Carolyn's hair. It was getting colder every day. "Can we go inside someplace to do it?"

Joy suggested the bookstore, and they hurried down the street.

Maya took a copy of the *Village Voice* from a pile of free newspapers at the entrance to the mega bookstore. Joy brought them to a quiet corner in the art book section and they sat on the floor. "I used to come here to do my homework when I lived at my dad's," she said.

"To get away from the crying baby?" asked Maya as she opened the newspaper and laid it out in front of them.

Joy handed her a red pen. "Exactly."

"Now, what are we going to write?" Maya asked.

"Something clever and ironic," suggested Joy.

"But he was so sincere in his note," protested Carolyn. "Shouldn't we be?"

"You want it to be sweet?" asked Joy.

"Yes," insisted Carolyn. "Sweet."

Maya tapped her hand with the pen. "Okay, sweet but formal. A formal letter accepting his formal apology. That would be funny."

"But it will be on newsprint instead of fancy paper," exclaimed Joy. "Perfect irony."

"Carolyn, you make it up," suggested Maya.

"Yes!" exclaimed Joy in agreement. "Just tell us how you'd write a *nice* letter accepting Serge's apology."

"You're using my sincerity for your irony," protested Carolyn.

"And your sweetness," added Joy.

Maya saw a look of worry cross Carolyn's face. She leaned toward her and tapped heads. "We're only asking you to do it because we love you, CK. We love you *because* you're sweet."

"And because you're a good sport," added Joy.

Carolyn thought, I'll write a letter that's super-formal. More formal and sweeter than anyone in her right mind would write. I'll show them irony. And maybe Serge will even get the joke.

She dictated and Maya wrote. DEAREST SERGE: WE HAVE RECEIVED YOUR APOLOGY AND READ IT WITH

GREAT INTEREST. WE HAVE DISCUSSED THE CURRENT, DIFFICULT SITUATION WE ARE IN WITH YOU. AFTER MUCH DELIBERATION, WE HAVE TAKEN A VOTE AMONG OUR-SELVES. THE VOTE WAS UNANIMOUS IN YOUR FAVOR. YOU, SERGE, ARE FORGIVEN. WE WILL BE PLEASED TO REMAIN IN YOUR ACQUAINTANCE AND LOOK FORWARD TO MEET-ING YOU UNDER HAPPIER CIRCUMSTANCES IN THE NEAR FUTURE.

YOURS MOST SINCERELY,

MAYA JOHNSON, CAROLYN KUHLBERG, JOY BENOIT-COHEN

"Brilliant," said Joy.

An hour later, Carolyn unlocked the door to her apartment. Her dad had been home for three days. She was glad to be back with just him. She'd missed him. She even missed their little apartment. He'd brought her beautiful gifts from Thailand — a red silk robe and slippers and two great scarves. And since he was back, he was giving her even more freedom. She could do neighborhood errands alone now.

She heard the radio on in her dad's room. "Hi, Dad," she called as she put her backpack on the kitchen stool. "I'm —" The word *home* caught in her throat. Photographs were spread all over the kitchen counter.

Carolyn dancing with Alex.

Carolyn's arms around Alex's and Serge's shoul-ders.

Wren and Alex kissing.

The pictures of Ivy were there, too. *Ivy playing her pots and pans. Ivy in her apartment.*

Thoughts rushed through Carolyn's head. Now her father knew she went to a party in a miniskirt and dyed her hair. Now he knew there were guys at the party. He could see that she'd been to Ivy's apartment. Without telling him. How would he punish her? Would he send her back to Wyoming? How had he gotten her photos?

Her father was at the counter now, standing over her, asking questions. "Where was this party?" "Were there any adults present?" "Did Maya's mother know where you were?" "What else are you keeping secret?"

Instead of answering his questions, she said, "You went through my things." She wasn't afraid anymore. She was angry. "Did you read my diary, too?"

"Carolyn, I am responsible for you," her father said in his most serious tone. "I discovered that you lied to me about Zeus. It's not a hairdressing salon. It's a tattoo and piercing parlor. And you knew it. So I checked your room to see what else you were hiding from me."

"You could have asked me," she protested.

"I asked you about Zeus and you lied." He pointed to the photo of her and Alex dancing. There was a portrait of Joy on the wall behind them. "I can see for myself that this party was at Joy's."

Carolyn nodded.

"Was her mother there?"

Carolyn shook her head no. She felt a lump rising in her throat. I will not cry, she commanded herself. I will not! She swallowed hard and blinked.

"Does Joy's mother know that boys were at the party?" He pointed to Serge and Alex. "These boys?"

"I don't know. I don't think so. They crashed the party," she answered in a rush. "We made them leave."

But her father wasn't listening. He'd already picked up the phone and was at the refrigerator looking for the Benoits' phone number on their most-used phone numbers list.

Joy was in the kitchen talking to her mother when the phone rang. Her mother picked it up.

"Who is this?" Joy heard her say. "Well, I don't understand, Mr. Kuhlberg. Of course I knew she was having a party. It was just a sleepover for three of her friends."

There was a long silence in the kitchen while her mother listened. Joy wanted to leave the room. Leave the apartment! But her mother held her with a look.

"I will not speak to you about this matter until I've spoken to my daughter. Good evening." She hung up the phone and turned to Joy. "Carolyn's father said there were three people *of a disreputable sort* at your party and that two of them were boys. He apparently knows this because he has seen photos — photos taken in this apartment. What is this all about? And who are these boys? Not from your school, obviously."

"I didn't invite anyone but Maya, Carolyn, and Jay-Cee," Joy explained.

Her mother's eyes were fiery, but she didn't raise her voice. "Well, that explains everything, doesn't it? Joy, tell me what happened."

Joy told the story of the party crashers coming up with the pizza guy and how she thought it would be two of Maya's friends who'd just dropped by. That they did know Serge, Alex, and Wren because of Maya's photography project. And that, after a while, she had asked them to leave and they did. She skipped the part about the attempted theft. She hoped that Carolyn had, too.

"I should have told you, Mom," Joy concluded. "I was going to, but I kept putting it off. I'm sorry."

"I am so disappointed in you, Joy," her mother began. As the scolding continued, Joy's thoughts turned to Carolyn. Her father must have found the pictures of the party. My mother will be mad at me, she concluded, but she probably won't punish me. She never does. But Carolyn will be punished for sure. Will her father forbid her to be friends with me? Is that stupid party going to be the end of our friendship? Will he send her back to Wyoming?

"If I can't leave you unsupervised, you'll have to go back to your father's so his twitty wife can keep an eye on you," her mother was saying.

The phone rang.

"If it's that man again, you're going to talk to him," her mother said before answering.

But it wasn't Carolyn's father. It was Maya's mother.

"If you don't mind," Joy's mother said into the phone, "I'm going to have Joy handle this, since she is the one responsible." She handed Joy the phone.

Maya's mother was waiting for her in the front parlor when she and Shana came back from the video store. "Come in here, please, Maya Johnson," she called in her strict-mother voice. Maya went in. Shana followed.

"I need to speak to Maya alone, Shana," Mrs. Johnson explained.

Shana sent Maya a sympathetic look. "I'll bring the videos upstairs."

"Tell me about Joy's party," her mother directed.

When the interrogation and lecture were over and sentence had been passed, Maya went up to her room. Shana was sitting on the bed playing Candy Land with Hannah. Maya had a flash of memory. When she and Shana were Hannah's age, they'd played that very same game on that very same bed.

She sat next to Shana and whispered, "I'm grounded for two weeks."

"Why?" asked Shana.

Maya put a finger to her lips and glanced at Hannah. When the game was over and Hannah had left to find another partner, Maya told Shana about the party. "I'm really worried about Carolyn," she concluded. "Her father is so strict. I'm afraid he'll make her drop out of the workshop. He probably won't let her hang out with me and Joy anymore, either. He might even send her back to Wyoming."

"It'd serve her right," said Shana. "She should have hidden those pictures better."

"How can you say that?" protested Maya. "It wasn't her fault. If it's anyone's fault, it's mine. I had a bad feeling about that party. Like I did about that boy who broke his arm in third grade."

"Richard?" asked Shana.

Maya nodded. "Remember how, when we were going outside to recess, I told you I had a feeling something bad was going to happen?"

"Well, no one broke an arm at Joy's party, did they?" Shana said with a laugh.

"You're not getting the point, Shana," said Maya. "I'm saying I should have listened to that feeling about the party and I didn't. All I cared about was having a good time and taking pictures."

Shana was glaring at Maya.

"What?" Maya said. "I used to be able to talk to you about this stuff."

"I'm supposed to care about your white friends and their big-deal party?" Shana said angrily. "You invited Jay-Cee. But you didn't invite me and Delores. That was the mistake. If I had been there, I'd have known that Wren girl was bad news from the moment I met her. I wouldn't have needed any *special feeling* to know that. I wouldn't have let her out of my sight."

"You're angry at me," said Maya in amazement. "Lately, you're always angry at me."

"Only since you been hanging out with the wrong people," explained Shana. She got up from the bed. "And you know what? I don't care about your stupid friends, or your so very precious photography class, or YOU." She picked up her backpack. "I'm going home."

"Shana, wait," Maya pleaded as she followed her.

Hannah came running down the hall carrying the portable phone. "Mama said there's a telephone call for you. She says it's Carolyn." Hannah held out the phone to Maya.

Maya looked from Shana to the phone. But she didn't have to make a decision about which friend to talk to. Shana was already on her way down the stairs. Without saying good-bye.

Maya took the phone from Hannah and went to her room.

"What happened, Carolyn?" she asked. "How'd he find out?"

Carolyn told her about her father searching her room and finding the pictures.

Maya lay back on her bed and dangled her legs over the side. "Is he furious?"

"At first he was. He was going to send me back to Wyoming. But now I think he's mostly sad because I haven't been telling him things. Like about photographing Ivy. My father called your mother."

"What'd she say?"

"She said she knew that Joy's mother wasn't going to be there until late," said Maya. "She kind of took responsibility for letting us go. I'm grounded for two weeks, but I can stay in the workshop."

"Me, too," said Carolyn. "I guess she told him being grounded for two weeks was a good enough punishment."

"That's all?"

"I'm going to have to report into him more. You know, take his cell phone everywhere, like before. And he made me promise to be more honest with him." Carolyn's voice lowered to a whisper. "I gotta go. He's back from the store. Tell your mother thank you." She hung up.

Maya looked around her room. The videos she and Shana were going to watch were on the bureau. There was also a neat row of manicure supplies, including nail extensions that Shana had brought for them to try. But Shana was gone. They weren't having a sleepover. Not now. Maybe not ever.

She rolled over and saw Hannah standing in her doorway with the Candy Land game. Maya patted the bed with one hand and motioned her little sister to come in.

Rockefeller Center

Being grounded meant two things for Carolyn. She had to go right home after school, and she couldn't leave the apartment on the weekends — except with her father. On the Sunday of the second weekend, her father took her to a movie. After the show they went into a café for take-out coffee and hot chocolate.

As they were leaving, her father stopped in front of the community bulletin board. It was covered with notices. He pointed his coffee cup at an announcement for a concert. "Isn't that your friend the dog walker?" he asked.

Carolyn studied the notice. It was for a concert at the Cathedral of St. John the Divine. There were pictures of two featured performers. One of them was Ivy, banging her pots and pans.

"It *is* Ivy," agreed Carolyn.

"Saint John's has musical events of a high quality," her father said thoughtfully. He was peering at the picture of Ivy. "And there's your name, Carolyn — along the side. It's small, but I can read it. You took that picture." He sounded proud.

Carolyn recognized the photo now and saw her

credit, too. "It *is* mine!" she said excitedly. "Ivy said she might use one of my pictures."

"Very impressive," her father mused. He pointed his cup at the other photo. "I know this Paul Winter's music," he said. "He plays a great soprano saxophone. And I've heard of this concert. They have it every year. It's to celebrate the Winter Solstice — the shortest day of the year."

Carolyn couldn't stop grinning. Her photograph on a flyer! Hundreds, maybe thousands of people would see it. She couldn't wait to tell Joy and Maya.

"We could go to this concert," her father was saying. "Would you like that?"

"Yes! I would." She moved to make room for two couples coming into the café. It was getting crowded.

"I suppose you'd like to invite Maya and Joy," her father added.

"Oh, Dad, that'd be so great. They both love the Big Bang Band. And that cathedral. You'll love it. It's so beautiful. Maya took me there last summer."

"I remember," he said. "So it's settled. It'll be my holiday gift. To you and your friends."

They *are* my friends, thought Carolyn. She was still smiling.

Maya spent the last evening of being grounded in her grandmother's ground-floor apartment. They sat at the kitchen table working on Josie's holiday cards. The cards were sky blue. Josie was painting silver angel wings on the front. Maya's job was to print PEACE in big gold letters on the inside of the card.

"Gran," said Maya thoughtfully. "Is it because I'm an Aquarius that I sometimes get these insights?"

Josie looked up from her work. "What kinds of insights?"

"Warnings about bad stuff," answered Maya. "Before it happens. They just pop into my head."

"Give me an example," she said.

Maya described the bad feeling she'd had about Joy's sleepover party. "And I was right," she concluded. "Bad things did happen and are still happening because of that party. Like Carolyn and me being grounded. And they keep happening."

"What do you mean *they keep happening*?" asked Josie. "This is the last day of you girls being grounded. And you told me Joy got her ring back."

"It's about Shana," answered Maya. She explained how angry Shana was about not being invited to the party. "Maybe the bad feeling was a warning about Wren stealing, us getting in trouble, *and* Shana being angry." She paused before adding quietly, "Gran, how did I know something bad was going to happen?"

"You're psychologically smart and alert to their feelings," answered Josie. "You know Shana well enough to know that she'd be upset about not being invited to that party. You said so yourself. That explains most of it."

"Most of it?" Maya asked. "What's the rest?"

"Seriously?" asked Josie.

Maya nodded.

"You sense things that other people might not pick up. But that doesn't mean you're responsible for everything that happens. Or that you're always right."

Maya shook the gold pen and opened the next card. "What am I going to do about Shana? She's so jealous of my new friends."

"Shana the scorpion," Josie observed. "She is strong-willed and can be hot-tempered. A powerful girl and loyal." She put a hand out and patted Maya's arm. "You have to be patient with her, dear, and patience is not *your* strongest quality."

"But what can I *do*?" asked Maya.

Josie loaded her brush with paint. "I just told you. Be patient. And keep your heart open."

Maya pointed the gold pen at her. "That's all?"

"You think that's easy?" answered Josie. She smiled lovingly at Maya. "Let's work quietly for a bit. I want to think about my friends while I make cards for them."

Maya wrote a gold P for peace on the next card. P is for patience, too, she thought. And parties. It's also for photography. Maybe I'll make cards. Only I won't paint them. I'll use an original photo — like Grandpa used to do. But which one? All I've shot lately are the piercing parlor and Joy's party. Not exactly what you'd want for a holiday card.

What's a symbol of the holiday season that's totally New York City? she wondered. The answer came in an image. The Christmas tree at Rockefeller Center! That's it. I'll photograph the tree all lit up. It'll make a great card.

"Remember all the lovely cards your grandfather and I sent out," Josie mused. "They always had one of his photographs."

"I remember," Maya said.

She didn't bother to tell her grandmother that she'd just been thinking of those cards herself. She was sure Josie already knew that.

Carolyn had a window seat on the bus going home from school. An elderly man sat next to her. A woman with two small children was in the seat in front of them. All of the seats were taken and several passengers were standing, including two men with briefcases. At the next stop, three noisy teenage boys in private-school jackets got on and pushed one another to the back.

A cell phone rang. The woman in front of Carolyn pulled a phone out of the diaper bag. Carolyn realized she'd forgotten to turn her father's cell phone back on when she left school. If he tried to call and she didn't answer, he'd be worried. And she'd be in trouble again. When she turned the phone on, the message icon flashed. Her father must have been trying to call her.

But it wasn't a message from her father.

It was from a woman. The message said, "Darling, I'm taking an earlier flight. If you can get away, meet me at my place at seven. I'll leave a message at your work number, too. I've missed you."

Someone called the wrong number, thought Carolyn. She was glad that the woman left a message at "darling's" office, too. She deleted the message.

Her father was home by five o'clock — an hour earlier than usual. "I have to go back to the museum tonight for a couple hours," he announced. "Work really piled up while I was gone. We'll have to eat dinner early."

Carolyn put aside her homework and they went to the kitchen. She cooked veggie burgers while he made a salad. She didn't mind that she'd be alone for the evening. It meant she could play loud music and lie around the living room doing her homework and talking on the phone with Joy and Maya.

When they'd finished dinner, her father announced, "I think I'll change into something more comfortable before I go back to the museum."

"I'll do the cleanup," she offered.

A few minutes later he came out of his room in his new jeans and a gray-green sweater.

"I like your sweater," she said. "Is it new?"

"I bought it in Thailand," he said.

She looked from the sweater to his eyes and back to the sweater. "It matches your eyes." A flash of memory. Her mother picking out a tie for her father and saying, "Gray-green. It matches your eyes." She wondered if her father was having the same memory. Dad must miss her so much, too, she thought.

"Where's the cell phone?" he was asking. "I'll take it so you can call me if you need me for anything."

After she gave him the phone, she remembered the wrong number call for "darling." She was going to tell him about it, but he was already out the door.

As Carolyn turned on the dishwasher, a question popped into her head. Why did her father take the cell phone? He never took the cell phone when he went back to work at the office at night. He had a phone in his office.

Another question. Why was he wearing a brand-new sweater if he was just going to be alone in his office?

She ran to the window and looked down to the street. He was heading in the opposite direction from the museum. If he wasn't going to the museum, where was he going?

Carolyn remembered the cell phone message. Maybe that call wasn't a wrong number. Maybe the message was for her father. *If you can get away, meet me at my place at seven.*

How could Dad have a girlfriend? she wondered. Doesn't he miss Mom? It wasn't like they were divorced, like Joy's parents. They were happy. He had adored her. I never thought my father would be with another woman. But he is.

He lied to *me*, she thought with a jolt.

She went into his room to look for more clues. A framed photo of her mother in her wedding dress was on the bureau. Beside it was a photo of her mother on horseback, with little Carolyn on her pony. She searched his dresser drawers. All she found were his neatly folded clothes. The drawer to his nightstand didn't hold any clues, either. But his suit pocket did. The clue was a shopping list they'd made out together on the weekend. Under the groceries her father was going to pick up, he'd added, FLOWERS FOR M. G.!

She heard a clicking noise. Was that the front door unlocking? Would she be caught in the act? She stuffed the list back in his pocket and ran out of the room, thinking of an excuse fast — a lie, really — for what she'd been doing in there. But it wasn't the door she'd heard. It was the dishwasher moving into the next cycle.

A creepy feeling spread through her. Her father had a girlfriend. "M. G." She was sure of it now. A girlfriend he sent flowers to. A girlfriend who called him *darling*.

He's been keeping it a secret from me, she thought. What would happen if I told him I knew?

The answer came to her in images. Her father introducing her to M. G. The three of them going to the movies together. M. G. coming to the apartment for dinner. M. G. inviting Carolyn to go clothes shopping. M. G. wanting to take her mother's place in their lives.

No. No. No!

I can't let him know I know, she decided. But I have to talk to someone about it. Someone who knew my mother. She sat on the couch and punched in Mandy's phone number.

*   *   *

Joy was on time for her father's birthday party. She'd been afraid she'd be late. It had taken forever to pick out the frame for the photo she was giving him, which the clerk had gift-wrapped. Slowly.

Maya took the photo that went in the frame. It was a medium shot of Joy in front of the Youth Media Center. Joy hadn't told her or Carolyn that the only photo of her in her dad's office was from when she was in the fourth grade. But when they were talking about what Joy would give him, Maya suggested giving him a framed photo for his office. She'd said, "You look so different from the way you did just last summer. You should give him a picture of how you look now. I bet the one he has is old."

Joy agreed that it was, and Maya offered to take the picture.

Carolyn had suggested she give him the Big Bang Band CD. That gift Joy had wrapped herself.

She rang the doorbell to her father's apartment. How long had it been since she'd been there? Six weeks? Or was it two months?

Sue opened the door, but it wasn't Sue she noticed. It was Jake.

He wasn't in Sue's arms.

He wasn't sitting in his jump-up-and-down swing thing.

He wasn't crawling around on the floor.

He was standing by himself — and walking. Toward her.

Her father had told her when Jake took his first steps. But she hadn't thought much about it. Seeing him upright surprised her. He looked like a person. A small person.

"It's Joy," exclaimed Sue. "It's your sister."

Jake was coming toward Joy so fast she thought he might fall. She squatted and put out her arms. He ran into them, laughing. She picked him up.

"Hi there, Jake," she said. "How's it going?"

"Ba-ba-ba," he answered.

Dinner was grilled fish, rice, and salad. Jake, now sitting in his high chair, had spaghetti with red sauce.

Joy took out her camera.

Jake, squishing spaghetti into his mouth with both hands. Click.

Sue asked Joy about the photography workshop. She explained Carolyn's project of shooting Ivy.

"Tell Sue about what *you're* doing," her father encouraged. "I think it's very interesting."

Joy explained her project.

"I agree with your idea, Joy," Sue said enthusiastically. "That's why I pay so much attention to how I look."

Not exactly the point, thought Joy.

"You're such a serious and thoughtful person, Joy," Sue was saying. "I admire that about you."

Joy said thank you, in case it was a compliment.

Joy and her father cleared the table for dessert while Sue cleaned up Spaghetti Boy, the high chair, and the floor.

There was an angel food cake for the birthday boy and no ice cream. "We all have to watch our waistlines," explained Sue. "Especially as we get older."

Dad likes chocolate cake way more than any other kind of cake, thought Joy. She'd be sure they had chocolate cake for dessert the next time they had dinner together — just the two of them.

Dad blowing out the candles on his cake. Click.

Dad unwrapping a present. Click.

He loved Joy's framed picture. "My Joy," he said. "You look so grown-up here."

"I'll put it on the piano with our other family photos," said Sue. She was already standing, ready to take the picture from him.

He clutched it to his chest. "Oh, no you don't. This is for my office. Things are rough around there these days. I need my Joy." Next he opened the CD. He studied the cover. BIG BANG BAND was printed over and over around the middle of the CD case.

"I've heard of these guys," he said. "I'm sure of it."

"They're all girls," said Joy, correcting him. "I'll put it on."

Jake, who was practicing walking around the living room, stopped when the music came on.

Jake standing in the middle of the room, listening to music. Click.

Jake bouncing, moving his arms up and down. Click.

His father swept Jake up in his arms and moved with him to the music. Sue joined in.

Dad, Sue, and Jake dance. Click.

Her father handed Jake off to Sue.

Dad dancing toward me. Click.

He reached for Joy's hand. "May I have this dance?"

May I have this dance? thought Joy as she joined the dancing. It sounded like something Carolyn's grandfather would say.

She started to laugh as they danced. Laughed because her dad was dancing so funny. Laughed because she was happy.

As they danced around the room, her father enclosed her, Sue, and Jake in a hug. "Thanks for the great birthday."

Jake put his arms out to Joy, and she danced with him through the rest of the number.

When the next song was over, Sue turned the volume down on the stereo and announced that it was time to put Jake to bed. "You have your workshop downtown tomorrow," Sue reminded Joy. "So why don't you sleep here tonight?"

Joy remembered that her mother was coming home late from a shoot in Long Island. She imagined going out into the cold night, finding a cab, coming into an empty apartment. She had her camera with her. And the mystery novel Paget had lent her.

"Okay," she agreed.

"Terrific," said her father. "I'll make pancakes in the morning. To celebrate that Joy is here."

"Oy-oy," said Jake.

"He knows your name, Joy!" exclaimed their father.

"That's just baby talk," Joy said.

"He is saying your *name*," insisted Sue. "That picture of the two of you. The one you took in the mirror last summer. It's in his room. Whenever I change his diaper, I point to it and say your name."

"Still," protested Joy, "he hasn't seen me in so long."

"Where's Joy?" Sue asked Jake.

He turned one-hundred-and-eighty degrees in his mother's arms to face Joy. "Oy-oy," he said as he put out his arms for her to take him.

And she did.

Maya was waiting for Joy when she came into the workshop the next day. "Are you busy after the workshop today?" she asked.

"Not particularly."

"I'm going to Rockefeller Center to take pictures of the tree. For my Christmas card. I thought maybe we could go together. It might be fun."

"Sure," agreed Joy. "What about Carolyn?"

"Her father actually said she could, but she has to be home by six-thirty."

The three friends left the media center together after class.

"We have to hurry," Maya explained as they fast-walked to the subway station. "It gets dark early. I want to take some pictures with the sky all blue and pink at sunset. And then some with the night sky."

"Have you been to Rockefeller Center yet?" Joy asked Carolyn when they were crowded into the subway car.

She shook her head. "But I've seen pictures of it. I watched the tree-lighting thing on TV. People ice-skate there. Right?"

"Right," said Joy. "You get an A-plus in tourism."

"You're the teacher," Carolyn shot back, grinning.

Joy found a seat, and Maya and Carolyn put their packs on her lap.

If Beth gave grades in the workshop, I wonder if I would have gotten an A, thought Carolyn. When she showed her final project in class, Beth had said, "Excellent work. You've shown Ivy in three different roles."

Charlie had commented that Ivy seemed like someone you'd like to be friends with.

"She is," admitted Carolyn.

Maya knew that some of the kids in the workshop were grossed out by the photo of Alex's tongue being pierced. Beth had asked, "Why did you choose to take that picture in extreme close-up?" Maya had told her that she wanted it to show something people might not otherwise see.

"I like it," Janice had commented. "It's strong."

"Did he have his tongue pierced to get that girl to dig him?" someone asked.

"Yes," Maya and Joy had answered in unison.

Joy was thinking about the workshop, too. She wondered if the class really liked her project. She'd purposely made the photos grainy and a little off center. "Why'd you do that?" Beth had asked.

"To make the photos look like a detective took them," answered Joy. "I was sneaking around, spying on the action. I wanted the photos to show that."

Beth nodded. "Good," she'd said simply. "Very good."

Now the workshop was over and the three friends stood in front of the lit tree at Rockefeller Center. Crowds of tourists were coming and going, oohing and aahing. Below them, the gold statue of Prometheus was bringing the gift of fire to humankind. The skating rink was in front of the statue and tree.

The excitement of it all sent a thrill vibrating up and down Carolyn's spine. While Maya and Joy took photos of the tree, she leaned over the rail and watched the skaters. She'd have to tell her father about this place. Maybe they'd go there together. She remembered M. G. with a jolt. Her father had a girlfriend — a "lady friend," would be the way her grandfather would put it. Her father was forgetting her mother.

Mandy said it was sad. She was upset for Carolyn. But she didn't have any advice. There were some things she didn't tell Mandy. Like, how she was mad at her father for going through her stuff, but that she'd done the same thing to his stuff. Maybe I'll tell Maya and Joy, Carolyn thought. They already know that Dad searched my room. Maybe they can help me figure out what to do. She wondered if she'd tell them how angry she felt at her dad.

Maya came up on one side of her. Joy on the other.

"Want to go skating?" asked Joy.

"Sure," agreed Maya.

"I only have a couple of dollars left of my allowance," admitted Carolyn.

"That's okay," said Joy. "I have enough money to treat. Both my parents gave me an allowance this week. They get confused about that sometimes. It's one of the advantages of being in joint custody."

They all laughed and raced to the elevator that would take them down to the skating rink.

While they were putting on rented skates, Maya thought about Shana. She and Shana had grown up skating together in Central Park. But they'd never skated at Rockefeller Center. She wondered if she should talk to Carolyn and Joy about the problems she was having with Shana. Maybe.

Joy, Carolyn, and Maya glided around the rink. Joy had skated here many times — always with her uncle Brett. She'd done so many fun things with him. Her first memory of fun alone with her uncle was of going to the merry-go-round in Central Park. How old was she? Three? Four? Suddenly, her thoughts turned from her uncle to her half brother. Jake walking into her room this morning, carrying a board book and shouting, "Oy-oy." Her name.

Maybe I'll be like Uncle Brett, she thought. I'll do special things with Jake, like taking him to the merry-go-round and ice-skating in Rockefeller Center.

The air was cold, but she was filled with a warm glow. Jake isn't going to be a baby forever, Joy realized. He'll be a person. My person. My brother. I'm not an only child anymore.

Maya's voice broke into her thoughts. "It's snowing!"

Joy looked up. Big fluffy flakes were tumbling toward her face. She stuck out her tongue to catch some. Maya and Carolyn copied her.

Carolyn skated backward in front of them and made a slow turn. Bright colored lights on the tree twinkling through polka dots of snow. Gray skyscrapers against the sky. She threw her arms out and shouted, "Winter in New York!"

Maya grabbed Joy's hand. "Come on. We'll give you a ride."

Carolyn took Joy's other hand.

I'm in the middle, thought Joy. She put her feet side by side and let her friends pull her around the rink.

Three friends laughing. Click.

Jeanne Betancourt lives and writes in New York City. She has written more than sixty books, including *My Name Is Brain Brian*, *Ten True Animal Rescue Stories*, and the popular Pony Pals series. Jeanne's work has been honored by many Children's Choice Awards. She is also an award-winning scriptwriter and has taught filmmaking to teens.